S U S A N N A   K A Y S E N ' S

A S A ,
A S   I   K N E W   H I M

"I have always known what was essentially
wrong with him; I saw it when I met him.
It may even have challenged me. Now, I
see the element of challenge; then, as we
rose into that atmosphere of pure longing, which was as buoyant as Cape Cod
Bay at high tide, and where we bobbed
effortless and bathed in anticipation, everything was inevitable. Love as destiny.
The problem is, he has no soul."

ASA, AS I KNEW HIM

ASA, AS I KNEW HIM

Susanna Kaysen

VINTAGE CONTEMPORARIES

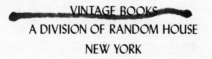

VINTAGE BOOKS
A DIVISION OF RANDOM HOUSE
NEW YORK

Fic

A Vintage Contemporaries Original, April 1987
First Edition

Library of Congress Cataloging in Publication Data

Kaysen, Susanna, 1948–
Asa, as I knew him.

(Vintage contemporaries)
"A Vintage original"—T.p. verso.
I. Title.
PS3561.A893A9   1987   813'.54   86-46186
ISBN 0-394-74985-5

Manufactured in the United States of America
10 9 8 7 6 5 4 3 2 1

For Ceil and Michael

ASA, AS I KNEW HIM

ASA ENTERS

Asa enters a room with his arms crossed. He slides in sideways and takes a pose against the wall. He looks as though he is at a cocktail party where he would rather not be. However, if someone enters a room where he is already ensconced (against the wall with his arms crossed, or in his own office in his red chair, long feet on the second rung of his typewriter table), he becomes hospitable: he uncrosses his arms. If standing against the wall, he arches his back and presses his shoulders to the plaster. This movement opens his breast, which is wide and padded, and outlines the flange of his ribs against his shirt.

Asa's shirts are blue or white. Asa's eyes match his shirts. On blue-shirt days his blue eyes beam reflected cobalt down paneled hallways; he has the smug aura of a handsome man. White shirts blank out his features so that his face is a white dish holding two dark marbles. On white-shirt days he is expressionless, a life-size photograph of himself snapped at a dull moment.

He is a man in middle age, of middle height and breadth. His ambitions have softened over the years, but without embittering him. He feels the weight of hope sliding off him slowly, easily—perhaps he was never meant to walk uphill. His straight line is all comfort: roses he has mulched and pruned, collars he has frayed in fifteen years at his desk, answering his phone. He no longer imagines himself a twenty-two-year-old. A few years back he realized that what was in the mirror had stopped surprising him. If his jaw couldn't put a crease in paper, what of it? He has peace of mind. He has two houses, he has three dogs, he has a red swivel chair at work, sound lungs, a slow heart, twenty-five more years with the roses.

Public Asa number one: the happy man. He uses it on days when he can't focus, or with people who need to be screened out. He can drop into it, slow bee-buzz of stability and contentedness insulating him from a female photographer with Boston vowels and a murky portfolio. It closes over him, the personality of a man stupider and more stolid yet kin to him—someone he could enjoy if, arms crossed, leaning against the wall, he were to chat with him at a cocktail party. "Nice fellow," he might tell Fay. "Dull but with a good heart. Told me all about his basset-breeding business. Fucking mopey dogs."

Asa's dogs are tall, springy, muddy: a speckled Airedale, and two standard poodles—one black, one brown. "Fighting dogs," he calls them. They are an extension, or accoutrement, of the happy man. Every evening they jump him and bang him into the oak coatrack by the door. Their smells and tight, dry hair delight him. They are other—not people, but living—and he loves them for their simplicity and sturdy presence. They love him for his warm hands, his shoes smelling of elsewhere, the growls he growls in their stiff ears after dinner, the way he comes home every day at six-twenty and waits to be jumped.

But he wonders if life could be like the life of the happy man. Life without the "slush," his name for that environment where he has not solitude, which he worships, but isolation. It isn't sharp, it's like mud, like February forever. He is slightly beyond the reach of life there. And life—the twilight crackling down on winter days, the book that kept him crouched on his elbow by the bedroom lamp till two last night—is visible, but nonsense.

To counteract this, and as a preventive measure to keep it at bay, he drinks more than he knows is good.

That's not why. It's a habit. His habit, after being jumped by dogs and kissed by Fay, is to drink some scotch, two glassfuls to be exact. One quickly and one slowly, while dinner takes shape behind a door. And on the nights when he makes dinner (public Asa number two: the aesthete), one quickly, one while making dinner, one while waiting for dinner to cook. One after dinner. And a refill. Maybe one more before bed. And a little to go to bed with?

He's thirsty. He thirsts.

He knows the names of all plants that have blue blossoms. He can sing, in a naïve and true baritone, the first movement of twenty Mozart symphonies and all the hymns he learned on snowy mornings in Connecticut more than thirty years ago. He can poach fish, bone chicken, make good coffee. He can splint a dog's injured leg, build a table, survive a night in the deep, booming woods. He enjoys calves' brains. He reads books that are of no professional use to him. He is capable of being moved (this means some escalation of his slow heartbeat, accompanied by near tears and a sense of loss, which is sweet) by the music he hears every other week in his hard season seat at Symphony. He likes to be alone.

When he is alone, he is not the happy man, not the aesthete, not, anymore, the well-bred young Cantabrigian, fresh and blond and sure of right and wrong—that person who no longer inhabits the mirror. He is tired. He is a tired man with less hair and energy than before. He daydreams. He puts his feet up and points his beaky nose toward whatever view is beyond the window. Then he signs off.

"What are you thinking?" asks Fay.

"Hm? Nothing."

Has he let go of life too early? He thinks of his father, a man with a similar nose and dissimilar mien—hard, rocky, dense and unknowable as his native New Hampshire. His father died at sixty-three. Asa remembers his father in middle age, when he, Asa, was solidifying the aesthete at Harvard. His father's presence was undimmedly strong; but probably, he decides, fathers can never lose that in their sons' eyes. And he was never sick, he just dropped. If he'd weakened—but he was over sixty and he didn't falter. Asa looks at the stretch of his legs from chair to windowsill, half in the sun. He is screened, he is cocooned in his disappointment, which lives below his every action and protects him. It's not a major sorrow, it's just the normal wear and tear of life on living things.

Some portion of beauty is in the possessor's knowledge of having it, and this Asa lacks. Still, he is beautiful; women warm up near him because he is fair and rosy and has an expansive chest where dream images of their heads lie, content. From behind he could be twenty-five, his back still a triangle racing straight to his haunches, tapered legs easy to imagine beneath the twill of his pants. He lopes, head forward, brown hands heavy at his sides; he moves as a cat moves in the morning, stalking small prey—no tension or excitement in it, only an impulse to move. He has the proud, large-featured head of an actor, but lacks an actor's poise. He doesn't know which profile is his better one. His face is full of flesh— wide mouth, heavy-lidded eyes, cheeks streaming florid to the softening under his ears. At the edge of his face age shows. In the middle, where his eyes tilt Eastern, exotic almonds of New Hampshire–lake blue, he is ageless—a sunburnt, scotch-ruddied Yankee with a blond beard poking through by 11:00 A.M. His head seems more ponderous than the body it lives on; when he slides down and tilts his red chair, half closing his eyes, it falls quickly to rest on the padded back. Thump. His chin points to the ceiling.

If there is a flaw in his appearance it is a lack of vitality. He has some sort of softness, not of musculature but of intention. This has its good aspect; he can, when comfortable, emit sensuousness. But he is so rarely at ease that the impression he usually gives is of sluggishness. There is something reptilian in his diffident, infrequent movements and tendency to bask in whatever sunshine makes its way into his office. That sharp-voiced, untalented photographer was sure he had slept through their interview. He knows he didn't, but he knows that people have found him intractably unexcitable. He has come to accept himself as such without wondering if the behavior is symbolic. "I'm just an average guy," he's said to friends of Fay's late at night. He hasn't got friends of his own. He says it with longing, but he doesn't hear the longing.

So, Asa Thayer. Do you see him? Can you hear the crackle of his shirt sleeve in the morning as he hangs his umbrella on the edge of the bookshelf? Could you have a pleasant conversation with him at dinner; do you know enough to know you don't want to?

I have always known what was essentially wrong with him; I saw it when I met him. It may even have challenged me. Now, I see the element of challenge; then, as we rose into that atmosphere of pure longing, which was as buoyant as Cape Cod Bay at high tide, and where we bobbed effortless and bathed in anticipation, everything was inevitable. Love as destiny. The problem is, he has no soul.

What makes him interesting is that he knows it. He doesn't know it's *that,* because he has no concept of the soul. But he knows he lacks connective tissue in a fundamental way. In terms of spiritual development, he is at the mollusk stage:

everything is backwards. There is the framework of his life—
Fay, flowers, his magazine, all those shirts stacked in the
drawer—which is only an external hardness of experience.
The inner experience, of slush and diffidence and self-deceit,
is gray, gelatinous, amorphous. But Yankees—they think this
hardness, these predictable concrete events that compose their
days, are the reality. It's a Protestant misconception. They
have no notion of symbol or duality or, most important,
passion.

I grew up with boys who were to become men of the sort
he is. They were blond and well formed, they came from the
large, ungainly families rich people have in periods of national
prosperity, they were beautifully educated and beautifully
mannered. And they were upright; the old, stern morality
still obtained in them. There were careers they would not
pursue—not so much out of snobbism as from an obligation
to "contribute," to give their ease and insight to society. Now
they are publishers and middle-level diplomats and heads of
progressive schools. I'm out of touch with them. Their first
names are Asa's middle name, or Fay's maiden name, and I
have been reminded of them, seeing Asa's checkbook open
on his desk with all those names: Higginson, Thayer, Bow-
doin. Old, stern Yankee names, on streets and buildings and
checkbooks from Long Island Sound to the Kennebec River,
names that sound like granite falling, like the ghosts of the
Wampanoag treading the pine-needle floor, like the coals
moving, settling down red in December, silver and hiss of
ash—Asa, Asa.

But for all the hardness and clarity of these names and these
values, their possessors are translucent, misty, soulless. There
is no blood in them. They are not connected to the past—
the human past—but to their heritage. They have great-
grandfathers buried beside earth reserved for their own dead

bodies and they have pewter utensils that are also soulless. They have forgotten the cave and the long night by the dying bonfire and the difficulty of chipping flint. They think their great-great-grandfathers sprang fully evolved on these shores, products of the *Mayflower*'s timber and New Hamphire rock. They've forgotten how to grunt—they've dismissed the possibility that anyone connected with them ever did grunt. They make love graciously, as if fencing.

Maybe I can't explain it. When I fell in love with Asa, I forgot he had no soul. No, not that: I believed he had a rudimentary one that lived in his perception of lacking it, and which I would nurture into a mythological beast, the Yankee with Blood. I wanted to give him this gift, passion. I wanted to make him alive. But he fought me; he even, for a while, transformed me into himself. All lovers experience this, the stronger absorbing the weaker and spewing him or her out remade, but I had thought I was the stronger. I am now. He is still bloodless; I survived him. I survived becoming him. Writing this is my last effort at transubstantiation. From his long, pale limbs I will make, by words, the body and blood of a human. If I fail, it can't be done. He sits across town in his red chair dismissing me; I am his happy memories. But isn't there yet in him something hot, some smoldering twig I left, which these pages can fan to fire?

As a story it's old and boring, probably the oldest, most boring one around. We worked together, we loved each other. He didn't leave his wife, I left my job. Living that story is living in a hurricane; that's why it is repeated until the listening population can no longer bear to hear it. As an experience it is beyond the norm, and those who experience want to tell . . . I'm not going to tell the story. At least, I'm not telling that story, but another, the skeleton, the essence within the story. But perhaps that isn't enticing either. After all, it's just a romance. We moved through rooms I could describe, talked with friends whose names you might want to know. Sometimes we took taxis—I think of kissing Asa in a taxi as we rode to the printer's, the pretense of a public embrace, the second-rate Boston skyline a backdrop for our little passions. Not little: They were a skyline all their own, the only view my eyes could see for years.

Now I have another landscape, which is life without him. He is not in the Chinese restaurant where we ate lunch on view weekly; he is not walking down the street when I am walking down the street, although he might be, and I hope he will be; he is not on the beach where I turn over and over in the sun, tanning my body for him to admire, but he never will admire it again; he is not on the sofa, in the chair, on his knees beside the bed kissing my wrists. I have a hole in my vision, and it's his absence.

But I know where he is. He is in his office at the end of a long dark hall. On his desk is a water glass gone cloudy from standing for an hour. From his tall, mahogany-framed windows he sees the same weather I see. Today, at ten-thirty, it is overcast, threatening August weather. The telephone with its bank of buttons is in front of him. My telephone is in front of me. We don't call each other. For me, not calling him is an activity. I know it isn't one for him. Once I would have convinced myself it was. My friends are glad that I know better now. My friends have hated Asa, first for monopolizing my mind, then for the endless discussions of him they were subjected to, finally, for making me unhappy. But they didn't understand what was at stake. The awakening of a soul is not a small matter; neither is the concomitant justification of my soul, my efforts. It's time to begin.

DINAH PROVIDES
BACKGROUND

My name is Dinah, which means "judgment." My parents, Adelaide and Frank Sachs, returned to the traditional names for their children. I have a sister named Leah and a brother named Seth. Now these names are fashionable; my married friends have children called Joshua, Jonah, even Obadiah. Thirty years ago our names set us apart and gave us an Orthodox aura that was at odds with our parents' determined atheism. But there we were, marginal, victims in grade school of the fascination certain kinds of Jews hold for Yankees. I learned early that I was to them some finer self, some more focused version of what they tried to be. They yearned for my historical sadness and intelligence. I yearned for their self-control and the inherited lawns where they had parties. I went to the parties—there wasn't anything that could be called anti-Semitism. It was more like the tension between the sexes; I was other, mysterious and full of power. Leah felt it too. She's married to a Swede, so it kept ahold of her. Rocked in that cradle of uniqueness by those blue-eyed boys, what protection could I have against Asa when, twenty years later, I looked up from my desk to find his huge head blocking my view?

Childhood was pleasant enough, judging from what my friends have told me of theirs. If my father preferred looking through his microscope to playing with us, I didn't blame him. He would park me, the eldest, in the reading room of Widener on Saturdays, with a stack of books on black magic (at eleven, my ambition was to be a witch), while he roamed the periodicals for the latest cellular breakthroughs. He must have made the journals himself occasionally—how else does one get tenure at Harvard?—but he was, and is, a small and dusty man, slightly vacant in his social interactions. He had none of the luminosity of his more famous colleagues who sometimes turned up for dinner. My mother was secretive. She had a room where she withdrew and did unknown things. Leah and I turned the furniture upside down and played Queen of the Castle while Seth burbled in his bassinet. My mother was probably tired of children and just sat in her room quietly reading Jane Austen. We didn't miss her. We were safe—we had enough to eat, each of us had a room with dire threats against trespassers posted on the door, we had bicycles, we had each other.

When I was thirteen I turned against witchcraft, having had a series of nightmares based on the activities of a wolf society in London that claimed membership of more than two hundred English werewolves (I had read about it in a book published only two years before, hence the nightmares), and took up the opposite sex. I dropped library research in favor of field work. I have been studying my subject for decades now, but it remains mysterious. Maybe, as my mother suggested when I was nineteen and my career had become clear to her, it isn't a topic worth devoting your life to.

"With all your gifts!"—the slogan of Jewish parents everywhere. But all three of us drifted. Most academic children do. The more successful the parent, the vaguer the child. We were lucky to have dusty, muddled Frank as a father. Leah has made a successful marriage, whatever that is, after an unpromising three years at art school. Seth earns a lot of money writing about how to program computers, and spends it on blondes, inevitable blondes, in restaurants without prices on the menu. And I, in my own way, am continuing my father's investigations into the origins of life. He doesn't see it that way, I know. But isn't the soul as vital as the gene?

Doesn't it bear scrutiny? Isn't the search for the Yankee soul as thrilling as Watson's hunt for that helix?

The male Yankee soul, that is. Asa's soul. I'll be honest. Until I met Asa I was merely amassing general data on males. I had found out that: They are hard outside but not always hard inside; they treasure women who make them laugh; they can change their personalities under the influence of a kiss received in a dark hall, a parked car, a side street. Some smell good, and for these I have an interminable lust; some smell odd—not bad but unbeddable—and make me nervous, as though we were not the same species.

Asa's smell (the fragrance of a beautiful man) is what I miss the most. I first smelled it three days after I had begun work at the magazine, when he leaned over my desk to hand me some papers, and the clarity of that mixture (rough, unfiltered cigarettes, fresh shirts, warm skin of a blond) alarmed me. My head snapped up to stare. He was in his persona of the happy, handsome man. Blue shirt, sleeves rolled up for the warmth of afternoon, gold and brown hairs shimmering on his arms, paper between his brown hands. Who was he? I remember sorting through the names and faces jammed into my head on the first day and coming out with the wrong answer—Roger Rowell, the editor. I didn't care if he were the janitor or the publisher, he was mine. I looked into his eyes; they were flat and awesomely blue, empty, receiving nothing. It was like looking into a portrait. Then he smiled and showed his crooked teeth, tinted with nicotine but well formed and healthy-looking. His eyes stayed blank through the smile. He put the papers on my desk and the movement agitated the smell, which surrounded his body like a halo, so that another gust of it came toward me. I had to shut my eyes. Like a virus his smell entered me and changed my cells, slowly, over years, until they craved only that smell, which was their oxygen.

The details. The names. The furnishings. It has a small staff, the magazine, and occupies a small brick house on a Cambridge side street, between a cobbler and a used-book store. Discreet gilt letters on one pane of the glass-paneled door identify it; I'll go one better and leave it nameless. Five of us acquired and edited the issue quarterly. The magazine verges on the scholarly. Roger and Asa like to think it is scholarly, but they know better. It keeps the sort of lawyer, doctor, or politician who regrets that he didn't get a Ph.D. slightly informed about a number of topics of no intrinsic interest to him, such as the newer understanding of fertilization in ferns or the controversy over the publication rights to T. S. Eliot's letters. As an endeavor it always seemed to me second-rate and fuzzy in outlook. But it was a grand place to work.

It was grand because Asa was there. To be all day in the presence of someone you love—I spent more time with him than Fay did. And it was a vital group, full of argument and feud, alignment and camaraderie. When an issue had just come out, we stumbled down the long mahogany halls like sleepwalkers, as if we had caught Asa's perennial drowsiness. There was time to quarrel about the content and layout of the next issue. Every combination of duos ate lunch together, discussing the characters of the other three. Whispers and confidences gave the workday a grade-school flavor. As publication drew near all this stopped; we became almost a unit, twenty arms and eyes focused on one objective. Almost, because Roger, the editor, thrilled to tight deadlines and inevitably slacked off at the penultimate moment in order to feel the full rush of adrenaline at the ultimate moment, when everything was due at the printer the next day and one article hadn't been written. Then he would take off his shoes and pad along the oak floor to the bathroom, where the claw-footed bathtub held competing periodicals, which he would read while sitting on the toilet—why? Revving himself into a frenzy of competition? Boom! Back to his typewriter, the article clattering out, a taxi coming at eleven at night to take the manuscript to the typesetter—we suffered under his mania for what Sally called "a photo finish." "We are working at an insipid quarterly," she said over one of those postissue lunches, "but Roger is the editor of the *Daily Planet*."

Sally was my confidante, my level-headed adviser, my mischievous encourager, my occasional doomsday prophet. Her views on my affair with Asa were always slightly out of sync with mine. But she held them firmly and told me every one. "He's not interested in you. He's got everything he wants and anyhow, he's barely interested in anything," she said one day, after his smell had been mutating in my bloodstream for more than a year. A week later she announced, "You're exactly what he wants. What forty-one-year-old man wouldn't want a beautiful young woman fawning over him?" Was I really fawning? "You look at him with a smirk on your face; you just can't get that expression of satisfaction off your puss," she answered.

"He smirks too," I said.

"More fool he."

We had these conversations in the fall. September was a hot, gold-and-umber month, and the warmth continued, supernaturally elongated beyond anybody's memory, into the start of November. On Halloween Asa's white cuffs were still rolled up to his still-brown elbows; he was still walking home at twelve-thirty to eat lunch on his back porch and maintain his tan. The vanity of middle-aged men—he knew his tan hid the broken veins in his cheeks and the scotch-spread of his nose.

On November 10, it snowed. I remember because it was the evening before my birthday. It was a high, blue, fluffy snowfall, leavened with warm air, rising a full foot on top of the piles of oak and maple leaves that edged the streets. I walked to work in the middle of unplowed streets, a thirty-year-old. I felt doomed, and irritated at feeling that because it was so predictable. But the snow seemed like a lid on life, the way turning thirty seemed. The world had stopped; it was just a static replica of itself, preserved in coldness. I was chilly and sad in my office, looking at gray papers in the milky light of a snowy day.

What was disturbing me more than anything was an erotic dream I had dreamed about Asa that morning, just before waking. It was so vivid (his tawny limbs moving against my white sheets, his smell saturating the pillows and my hair) that I had woken entirely excited. And in one of those flashes of insight that come between sleep and true waking, I had wondered why I was wasting my time on this impossible mission. For I was by then completely occupied in my siege of Asa's heart. I was set up in front of his fortified self with enough rations, in the form of obsessive thoughts and endless desire, for years. Nobody else interested me. What a way of putting it—I didn't even register other men on my eyeballs. They were grains of sand on the beach, and Asa was the ocean, an unplumbed blueness in which I was determined to swim. So I sat at my desk, still dizzy from my dream and half hoping he wouldn't walk in to say good morning as he always did, because I thought I might jump him and wrap my legs around his waist and push him onto the floor—and so forth. Of course, at the same time I was waiting for him, so that I could quickly graft the three-dimensional Asa onto the remnants of my dream and have a private swoon as I sat at my desk. My birthday present, wrested from him in secret.

He must have had a busy morning, because he didn't appear until almost eleven. He sat down in the chair opposite my desk—my interview chair, we called it, joking, for none of the women interviewed anyone. He crossed his arms and pushed himself back with his feet, so that his chin rested on his collarbone and his eyes were level with mine.

"I had a dream about you last night," I blurted. I often blurted things at him. He caused me to become overvivid, tensed until I was nearly parodying myself. I sensed that what drew him to me was my foreign approach to life. Foreign from his. I talk more than he, and about things he wouldn't discuss, and I cry, and embrace people when I'm happy. I found myself exaggerating all this with him, in response to some need of his to have it exaggerated.

"You did?" He shut his eyes and lifted his chin. "I had a dream about you too."

This was so stunning that I was momentarily quiet. I stared at him. He was smiling at me and nodding slightly, or maybe his drowsy head was wobbling.

"What was it?" I asked. My pulse was so noisy I was sure he could hear it.

"Oh, I'm not going to tell you. But it was full of warm, loving, tender feelings." And he looked at me with what he thought was a loving, tender gaze. It wasn't; it was an unmistakable grimace of lust and it made me panic. If he was going to capitulate this easily I would feel cheated. I was set up for a long fight, and I suppose I wanted one. I wanted the obstacles to be proportionate to the prize. At that moment, when I had been at the magazine barely a year, he was still my superior, my married boss about whom I had sexual fantasies. I hadn't separated him from his function. I couldn't see him simply as a man. So this evidence of his susceptibility to me, though thrilling, was too early. I began blurting again.

"I dreamed we were in a kindergarten, all sorts of kids running around, and there was a fire—was that it? Something—and I couldn't find you, then I saw you on the other side of the yard and I ran to you." I paused. "I ran up to you and right into your arms." I said this softly. I didn't look at him.

When I did look up he was still staring at me with his "tender, loving" look. We sat like that, staring, until Sally passed by my door on the way to her adjacent office. Asa heaved himself out of my chair and slinked into the hall.

"Goo, goo, goo," said Sally. I could hear her through the wall. Asa was halfway to his office, and as he's somewhat deaf he couldn't have heard her. Nevertheless it worried me. Now that the moment was over, it took on the slippery feel of fantasy. His desire seemed like something I had conjured up or talked him into. Sally's teasing heightened my sense of having manipulated the situation, making me believe I had something to hide from him and worried that he would "find out." If he thought I was plotting love attacks and, worse, checking my strategy with Sally, he might resist me to teach me a lesson. "Shut up," I said, loud enough for her to hear. I put my head into her office. "He's still walking down the hall."

"Oh, he's deaf," she said. Then she laughed. "What was all that goo about?"

"Erotic dreams. We were trading erotic dreams."

"Terrific. What was his?"

"No details. It was full of 'warm feelings.' "

"He'll say anything to you."

At first this pleased me; yes, he would say anything to get

my attention. But Sally had meant it dismissively, and, as I sat at my desk and pretended to work, I decided that he was just flirting with me. He would say anything because nothing mattered; it was all fantasy. Whereas for me it was real, a concrete advance. I was one yard closer to the ramparts. I jumped up and went into Sally's office.

"But I love him," I said. I was standing in the middle of the room and staring at her. She was the only person to whom I could say it. She had been that for so many months that some of my love had rubbed off onto her and I saw her as beautiful and precious. I wanted her to say, "I know," or "Of course you do," or anything that would make me feel my love was accepted. She had become a figurehead to whom I offered my gifts. But she wasn't one, she was Sally who'd been at the magazine for too many years, who was trying to get her work done, who was tired because her job was harder than mine and she had a child at home.

Simultaneously she was a Jewish woman who ought to be sympathetic. She'd married a Yankee rather late in her life, a man named Dickie Dana, and had thereby become a cousin of Asa's. They socialized a little; the Thayers invited the Danas to the Cape for a weekend every summer and the Danas had the Thayers to dinner once or twice during the winter. Asa borrowed tools from Dickie, who had a collection of saws, chisels, plumb lines, routers, even a miter box left to him by a black-sheep carpenter uncle who had built himself a cabin in Vermont in the twenties and died there in the sixties, during a winter so cold his body was frozen—wrapped in frozen sheets and blankets—by the time he was missed in town, which was only overnight. This uncle's habit (his name was, I think, Faneuil Dana) had been to ride his tractor into town every morning and take coffee with three other old farmers in the donut shop. They missed him. They finished their coffee and took somebody's truck into the woods to look for him, a few boards in the back in case they needed to make a coffin. They didn't bother to bring a Band-Aid, or even some brandy. Arrogance, or a morbid acquiescence? They used his tools to put the nails in.

Dickie had told me this story the night I met him, and it was obvious that he relished it, as a story. As I came to know him better, I began to understand some of its appeal—the studied eccentricity and need for solitude were qualities he had also inherited from his uncle. More important was the element of foresight, which I labeled acquiescence. For Dickie, this certainty the three old fellows had about what they would find in the cabin was delightful. "They knew!" he kept repeating, leaning across the table in his drafty dining room. "You see, they understood what had happened. And they were prepared." Dickie was trying to prepare himself for death as well. We must, and he's past sixty, but he has moved his perspective somehow, as though he's looking back at life from the other side. He's healthy, he looks to be in his late forties, and he spends his time "tidying up," "sorting things out," stripping himself of unnecessary objects and thoughts. He has some money, some old Yankee money, and Sally works.

What struck me about this story—and I think of it often, in connection with my research—was the cold. The cold outside, the cold living in the shack when no one else could live in it, the cold old men in the unheated truck bumping through the woods without a word. I hear Asa saying, "Oh, I don't feel the cold." They all say that. Do only Jews have skin and nerves? Sally and I spent ten minutes every morning discussing how cold we were, which parts of us were almost frostbitten on the way to work. Dickie stands on the front porch in January wearing his bathrobe, saluting the gray, rigid day with his naked chest. Are they made of stone?

That morning, when I stood expectantly beside the file cabinet containing the manuscripts for the previous issue, waiting for Sally to sympathize and tell me Asa's secrets, she instead put on a very good performance as a stone Yankee.

"Mmmmmm?" she said, not raising her head from Fowler's. "Mmmm." A well-bred invitation to get out.

So I got out. I shuffled back to my office and I resolved to declare myself to Asa. I wanted to confront him with what he was doing, which was making me fall in love with him. I wanted to move it away from fantasy and into reality. As long as neither of us admitted what was happening, it could continue. I was going to jeopardize everything, possibly, for the sake of flesh. I couldn't bear all the goo, the sidelong looks, the whispered comments during editorial meetings, the hand on my shoulder as he passed me in the hall, unless I had the substance. What I meant by the substance was the food of his flesh, his arms and face and back to lick and smell and twist myself around. I was willing to give up the flirtation if it didn't progress.

I was not. I was not willing to give up anything—but I was sure I would succeed. I felt his heat; he was and remains the only Yankee man who smolders. Maybe it was simply lust, even after these years of him I don't know, but he was warm with it, flushed from it, and I trusted that. I wanted to make a bonfire, at first. I made one, and then I wanted something else, a well-planned arrangement of kindling and a backlog, that would burn for years. But I am getting ahead of myself.

Sally, on the day I turned thirty, was past forty. We might have been sisters, and it would have been difficult to say who was the older. We are both small, dark women with smooth skin that doesn't wrinkle. Only her laugh reveals her age; it is sad, knowing, and short. I haven't learned enough about the world to have the sense of sorrow that curtails laughter. I don't have many clues about what made her sad. Perhaps getting what you want is saddening. Dickie too had been married when she'd met him.

I miss her and Dickie. Dickie was enthusiastic—ecstatic, actually—about my prospects with Asa. "He needs you to wake him up. You are a goddess, you will drag him into the waters with you," and so on. Then, gazing into my eyes, which I suppose reminded him of Sally's eyes ten years before, "I'm jealous of him." There was much of this while I was plotting my attack. They were my aides-de-camp; they knew the territory better than I did, and spread the maps out for me, and fed me dinners while I raved about my strategy. But when Asa kissed me, that black March evening when the world turned inside out, a barrier went up between me and the Danas. I had moved into another sphere. I was Asa's satellite, not theirs. I didn't need their maps because I had hard, inside information. I knew how he tasted, the sounds he made when I touched him in ways that he liked, the way his face looked when he was lying down. They knew what he and Fay had for dinner, and how much Julia's school cost, and where Asa banked his paltry salary. So we became estranged, in a civilized and subtle way. We had used each other up. I was too loyal to Asa and too single-minded to provide them with the tidbits that might have kept their vicarious interest up. And they, out of some other loyalty, perhaps to Fay, or perhaps just to the institutions of stability, were unwilling to give me ammunition for the next challenge, which was making Asa mine.

Besides Sally and me, who shared the duties of proofreading, copyediting, and organizing the flow of papers from typesetter through editor to art director, there were Roger Rowell, the editor, in his socks, and my enemy, Adrian Françoise Jessel. Adrian Françoise was Asa's assistant, which meant that her duties were not well defined, and that meant she put her nose into other people's duties. Her nose was long, pale, and refined; she was a long, pale, and refined-looking young woman. She had beautiful hands and tapered ankles and wrists. She was nearly a foot taller than Sally and I were, and had a number of inches on Roger and Asa as well. Like most tall women she slouched, but she moved quietly and deftly. She could be rummaging through my files before I heard her coming. That is to say, I never did hear her coming. What gave her presence away was postnasal drip, which made her sniff.

Adrian Françoise wasn't always my enemy. She evolved into my enemy. Competition for Asa put the finishing touches on a foundation of distrust and mutual incomprehension we had been building for about a year. We didn't have the same style, and we didn't have much charity for each other's ways.

To begin with, I couldn't bear her name. Adrian or Françoise would have been bad enough, but being compelled to say them both—and she did compel that. "Hello. I am Adrian Françoise," she said to me on my first day, giving equal weight to both names and pronouncing them without a pause in between. She had a suggestion of a French accent, more a deliberateness of intonation than any distortion of vowels, and that also bothered me. I felt that it was affected. I was sure that Adrian Françoise could speak normal American English if she chose to. She probably couldn't, but she provoked that sort of thinking in people. It was Adrian Françoise who dummied up the more boring articles that Asa didn't feel like dealing with, and she would come to me to check the changes she had made to lose or gain lines. Hers were never intelligent changes; she had a gift for torturing language. She was adept in using the passive. After I'd been there for a few months I started changing her changes, or making them before she got a chance to. That led to arguments over the cheapest way to lose lines. Adrian Françoise was also responsible for approving the composition bill and arguing with the typesetters (Asa being too well-bred to like dealing with money), and she had her eye on the penny.

"That change will cost $3.25. Do you really think it's necessary?"

"I guess not," I said lamely, for about half a year. Then I changed my mind.

"Yes. It's wrong as it stands."

"Then why didn't you change it in manuscript?"

"Well, I just missed it, or Sally missed it."

"Ohh. Mmmmm." Adrian Françoise could say "mmmmmmmm" in an extraordinarily vibrant way, owing to postnasal drip.

And so we had a permanent state of war over lines. I would change a line or two on the galleys, she would catch the galleys before they went back to the typesetter and delete or diminish my change, I would reinstate it on the page proofs, and she would appear in my office holding a grimy Xerox she had made of my misdeed and say, "I see you made that change . . ."

"What change, Adrian Françoise?"

But this sort of stuff is neither evil nor remarkable. More noteworthy, actually quite astonishing to me, was that Adrian Françoise went through our desks. She didn't only read everything on top of desks and hanging from bulletin boards, she went deep into drawers, into envelopes under pads of paper where one's paycheck stubs were, in the file farthest back, where one had little notes written by—well, in my case, Asa. It was Sally who figured out she was doing this.

"Aff [we called her this to save time, since we discussed her a lot] is going through my desk. She's probably going through yours too. So watch out," said Sally one grim December morning.

"How do you know?"

"I mentioned I wouldn't be in on Friday and she said, 'Oh, right, you're going to Chatham.' The only way she could have known that was from looking in my private calendar, which I keep in my right-hand drawer, in the back. I mean, you'd have to paw through the whole drawer to find it."

"What did you say?"

"I was so stunned I just nodded. I'm taking my calendar home. Nothing's safe here." Sally was stacking and unstacking her dictionaries and style manuals in an attempt to impose her will on something. "No fucking privacy."

"Not a fucking bit," I agreed. I loved the way Sally said "fucking." I often egged her on when she was irritated, just to get her to the point of swearing; it took a lot to make her swear, but once she started she was impressive. She said "fucking" as though it were spelled with seven initial *F*'s. "But," I continued, "you don't really have any secrets in your desk." I was thinking of my collection of notes from Asa. At that point they were entirely innocent: "Please see me about American history article, I need to lose a paragraph." "Where are book column galleys?" "Can't find manuscript we were discussing this morning, do you know where it is?" That sort of thing, not very steamy. Still, my keeping them was suspicious, and Adrian Françoise was smart enough to see that, if she'd found them.

"I want my private life to be private," snapped Sally. "I

don't want somebody checking up on my movements, when I'm having lunch with whom, what kind of crackers I have in my drawer, for Chrissake. I can't stand it. I want to wash my desk."

I took Asa's notes home that evening, and worried for a while over whether Aff had seen them. But she treated me no worse and no better than before, so I forgot about it. I continued to stuff my paycheck stubs into the back of my drawer, and to leave money among my pencils, and generally to behave as though I had no secrets either. Maybe I wanted to catch her out somehow.

Still, the desk incident occurred after the erotic-dream exchange, and Adrian Françoise, with her hypersensitivity and snoopiness, didn't miss the flirtation between me and Asa. I think it was in January, at the start of the decade, that our relations took on an edge that at first puzzled me. She began turning up in Asa's office when I was there. She was frequently sitting at my desk, in my chair, when I arrived in the morning, as if to declare herself a licensed snooper. Our arguments about lines got worse; she once turned on her heel (Adrian Françoise actually did things that I had hitherto only read about, such as turn on her heel and wring her hands) and stamped out of my office in the middle of my explanation for why I had decided to make a certain change. Then one day Asa called me on the intercom when Aff and Sally were in my office to tell me that Harvard radio had started their Mozart Orgy, and that I should listen. We (Asa and I) were Mozart fans, and much of our flirtation consisted of discussions of music and the trading of banal rhapsodies over Mozart, which were just disguises for rhapsodies over each other. "He's so elegant," I'd say, staring at Asa's immaculate shirt. "So delicate," he'd rejoin, his eyes on my arms and neck.

"The Mozart Orgy's on," I said, returning the receiver to its beige cradle. I turned on my radio.

"Was that Asa?" asked Adrian Françoise.

"Yup."

"Oh. He tells you, and then you tell us?"

"Yup," I said. I looked at her. "That's right." I felt like rubbing it in.

"Well. We must listen," said Aff. She made it sound like a duty. She rose, smoothed her straight skirt, and went to attend to the music.

"She's jealous," I said to Sally. "That's it, she's in love with him too."

"No. She loves him. You're in love with him."

"Big difference."

"There is. You know that." Sally had a trick of saying "You know that" in a sly, co-conspirator tone of voice that made me feel part of an elite. "Why shouldn't she love him? He loves her. Because of her he'll never have to cast off another manuscript about whale migration, or write another letter to the Bettmann Archive. She makes his life wonderful, and he rewards her with money. So she loves him."

Money. Women who want money don't work for second-rate, quasi-academic journals. Nonetheless, Sally was sure she was getting a raw deal. She had been there three times as long as Adrian Françoise, and she was older, with a family to support (Dickie's money was enough to maintain him in the style to which he was accustomed—scotch, lots of novels, raw hamburger for dinner, a month in Chatham at the family estate; it didn't cover dentistry or new tires or school clothes for Honor). Adrian Françoise made a good deal more money than Sally did. And it was as Sally said, because Asa would pay anything to get certain things off his mind and desk. Sally and I only insured that the magazine came out on time, without errors. Somebody had to do that, and people were trained to do that. Until Adrian Françoise turned up, nobody knew that there was such a thing as a person who would do unpleasant tasks efficiently, even with relish. Oh, Adrian Françoise was crafty. Her snooping and powers of observation had aided her in finding out all the things Asa hated doing and learning how to do them.

For Asa was the man with the money. He may have been too well-bred to want to deal with it, but he was capable of dealing with it, which was more than could be said of Roger. So it was to him that we applied for our raises, with our little tales about rent and oil prices. We didn't get them. We got cost-of-living increases: 3 percent, 4 percent if our performances had been diligent. Two weeks before he kissed me, he gave me a raise—an actual raise. Twelve percent. I didn't tell Sally.

It's almost grotesque, isn't it? It's such a seedy story. Were it not for the setting—the office shaded by elms, the eccentric, colorful characters, the challenging and intellectual nature of our work—this could be a story whispered in the corridors of a textile mill at the turn of the century. The boss, the young employee, her charms, his wily ways. She left in disgrace. . . .

I left because I couldn't watch him stomping on his heart and mine. That's all he was doing in the end. He loved me— he still loves me. I know love when I feel it, and I felt it from him. It warmed me through and through, to the coldest February-chilled marrow of my thigh, the secret cells in my blood. But sometimes it doesn't matter whether people love each other or hate each other.

I may have been born to love him—I'm sure I was; loving him was easier than eating or sleeping—but he was surely born to stomp on my heart. He was better at that than at loving me. He loved me because I was exotic, foreign, incomprehensible, and for those same reasons he justified expelling me from his life and mind. He is a member of a ruling class, and rulers must have subjects; but it's been more than a century since his aristocracy held power, so as a group they are softening, degrading—and these are mortal sins, for Yankees. Therefore, every opportunity to be upright, harsh, cold, and granitelike must be seized. And to temper that, there must be some nobility, some selflessness to prove that they have the right to be the ruling class. So I think Asa conceived of me as his colony; he protected me and nurtured me initially, then withdrew sternly, leaving me to fend for myself and congratulating himself on his honorable relinquishing of power. His word had been law (after all, who decided when we spent time together and how much time we had?), but he was not a tyrant; he knew when to loosen the link.

Is that what he thought?

Was he merely a coward, afraid of being caught? Were the half-truths and scurrying around Cambridge at lunchtime too much for him? Was it Fay, with her brown eyes looking into his every night? "You don't know what marriage means to a man like that," Sally said many times. "He loves comfort so. He's been married forever. He'll never give it up." I refuse to wonder if he loved Fay more than he loved me. What good can asking that question do? Not even he knows the answer. There can't be an answer. It's a question, really, of how he wants to live, and he has a way of living. It's his, his dogs, his oak thresholds, his history with her.

Even now I can't stop making excuses for him.

Adrian Françoise loved Asa and he was indebted to her. He treated her with a perfect, warm politesse he never extended to anyone else. They mythologized each other: She considered him a handsome benefactor and overburdened man of refinement whose welfare she was tending; he considered her an angel, a model of good-tempered efficiency, an unemotional woman. I'm sure that in her deepest sleep Adrian Françoise had locked limbs with Asa, but she didn't know it. She never turned up in his dreams—I know because I asked him. I was jealous of Adrian Françoise, probably because I never bothered being jealous of Fay.

("Oh, Dinah," said Asa, "she's so unjuicy." And placed his palms on my breasts. We had just gotten up from bed, at two-thirty in the afternoon, and stood naked, admiring each other, tracing the lines of sweat and liquid on each other's thighs.)

Their mythology created problems in the office. It made Asa ignore her bad habits and unwilling to hear about them. Sally took him out for lunch to describe the desk rifling. His response was, "Tell her to stop it." To me he said, "What can I do? What am I supposed to do? Should I talk to her?" This in a tone that pleaded with me to say exactly what I said, "No, no, darling, that wouldn't help." I said that because I didn't want a confrontation between them, for Adrian Françoise had gone crazy on the trail of our affair.

Of course she knew what was happening; everybody did. Sally knew because I told her. Roger knew—I've always wondered if Asa told him, bragging. He knew and he took to leering at me. One day he came into my office to ask me the generic term for a woman with whom a man is having an affair. I took up the challenge. "A mistress, Roger," I said with equanimity. "That's what I thought, but I don't like the way it sounds. Isn't there some other word?" Roger wasn't in the habit of coming to me for help with his problems. I stared at him. "Courtesan," I said. "Paramour." I watched him turning a bit pink. "Popsie." "I guess mistress will do," he mumbled, and padded back to his office. Charlotte the receptionist knew: Her lunchtime scorecard of people's ins and outs frequently read, "Asa & Dinah   ?" Entries for others read, "Roger   2:30."

Adrian Françoise was torn between wanting to prove it and wanting to pretend it wasn't happening. As our passions expanded, her eavesdropping and desk rummaging became more frenzied. At the same time, the expression on her face became fixed. There was a film over her eyes. When Asa and I went out for lunch together, which, after our kiss, we did once a week, Adrian Françoise would snag us at the top of the staircase to ask Asa questions that didn't need to be asked, and her face would be entirely clouded over with self-imposed confusion. She'd look from Asa, wearing his glasses and buttoned into an overcoat, to me, similarly buttoned, tapping my red boot on the carpet, and mystification would fairly leak from her eyes. But there was an urgency and determination in the way she kept us standing there, slowly unwinding her series of questions, wrenching from us a nugget of our most precious element, time.

Adrian Françoise did not know where to stop. She asked me lots of questions. First they were questions like, "Why did you and Asa have lunch last week? Were you discussing the new layout for the book feature?" To which I replied, succinctly, "No." Then she tried to be my supervisor, which technically she was. "Are you having some problems at work that you've been discussing with Asa? Is he giving you trouble about money? Maybe I can help." These sorts of questions soon gave way to trap questions: "Where is Asa this morning?" "When is Asa coming back from lunch?" "Is Asa taking Friday off to go to New York?" "At the dentist, two-thirty, yes," I would answer. I was bragging, but she had provoked me. Then she started to follow me around. She even told me she was doing it.

"I have to pick up some tickets for the Kurosawa film tonight, I'll stop by your house," or "I'll walk you home, I have to go to the post office." What she wanted was to catch Asa. He came to my house every day after work to neck with me. We spent months inching our way to bed, as if we were fifteen. He kissed my shoulders for one month and kissed my breasts through my blouse for the next month. At five-twenty he turned the corner of my street wearing his glasses, carrying his briefcase, head bent—ashamed, hiding his features? Up the stairs, the dangerous wait, exposed, until I answered the bell, then avalanches, earthquakes, everything disintegrating as we devoured each other in the hall, me pushing the door shut behind him, both of us alert to Cambridge poised behind the maple panels. "Was that Asa Thayer going up those steps?" Perhaps we were the only people who cared. No, Adrian Françoise cared. I knew she dawdled at the Brattle Theatre, reading the schedule slowly as she walked down the street, waiting for Asa to walk by. I don't know whether she ever satisfied herself by seeing him.

By the time she was doing this I felt safe, because Asa was guilty too, and that restrained her from overstepping all the bounds. She might, in a sanctimonious panic, have called Fay and started babbling, but the fact that Asa was compromising himself stopped her. He had failed her by becoming susceptible to me. Earlier I had feared her. When I lay on my sofa and thought about him on short February afternoons, I thought also of Adrian Françoise and how she was sniffing out my passion, how she would sniff it out before he did and tattle to him and jinx my chances. I could see her standing beside him, in his swivel chair, smoothing and smoothing her straight skirt, saying I was unprofessional, I was using sexual tactics to improve my position at the magazine. And you see, I didn't know what he was feeling then. I didn't know he was as infected as I. She terrified me.

Yet, with all the fear—and I feared not only Adrian Françoise but Fay, and Roger, and everybody on the street who could surely read my lunatic passion in my face—and the certainty that he would not acquiesce, I had just the opposite of these, and I was happy. I had a thousand moments of contact and exchange to fondle every evening, and I had the secret of his nascent soul. That was a secret even he didn't know. I knew it was the key to him. I knew I'd press against him and warm his soul into being, and I knew nobody could resist an opportunity of such hot, cosmic dimensions, not even Asa.

THE ANGEL OF
MONADNOCK
I

In 1955 Asa Thayer, a sixteen-year-old in the limbo between junior and senior years at Choate, spent his first summer in a decade at home in Cambridge rather than on his paternal grandparents' farm outside Concord, New Hampshire. Staying had been a triumph over his parents' insistence that he continue to help his grandfather chase chickens and turn, with large, corroded forks, the piles of compost at the bottom of the vegetable garden. Instead he was pumping gas at the edge of Harvard Square, in a station that issued inspection stickers without bothering to inspect. He made twenty-two dollars a week; he paid his mother ten, of which she banked five for his future and put five toward his board. "We cannot," she said at the start of June, "simply carry you as part of the household while you waste your time." He ate the eggs she cooked him every morning off blue Chinese plates plundered by a sea captain forebear; his bed, mahogany, with intricate and dusty pineapples on each post, had been the resting place for an infrequently remembered signer of the Declaration of Independence; when he walked down the stairs ancestors with noses and eyes like his watched from gilt frames. And the twelve dollars remaining to him on Fridays was the largest sum he had ever held in his back pocket.

The house was at the far end of Brattle Street. Asa's father, a doctor, could not afford to live the four or five blocks closer to the center of town that would have been appropriate to his lineage. But the rooms were large, high-ceilinged, and many. Better, even in mid-July they maintained a dim, cool atmosphere perfumed with oils rubbed into wood, dust settled on books, and died-down fires of hard, slow-burning, sweet branches. It was a house that in no way admitted to

the extreme seasonal changes of Massachusetts, as its inhab-
itants also ignored the fabulous February cold, the equally
fabulous August doldrums. Its furnishings suggested a permanent early winter, and in this it reflected the climate of the
three people who moved across the parquet floors.

It was a hot summer; the hoses ran all day on the lawns
along Brattle Street, and Asa biked through the black pools
collected at the curbs on his way to and from work. The hiss
of his tires toward evening, when the sun was still high, was
the whisper of the real evening, the dark evening coming,
when he would move to the edge of his chair and say, "May
I be excused?" His parents were propped like dolls at either
end of the table, silent with incomprehension. They knew
where he was going, they knew how he was spending his
time, yet his life had become mysterious to them.

"Be home by ten-thirty," his father ordered every night.

"Yes, sir," Asa answered. He came back at one or three,
when the stairs were a minefield of creaks and rattles.

"Going swimming at the Solas'?" his mother asked every
night.

"Yes."

But it didn't satisfy them. They were unappeased. Sometimes his father telephoned there—"We'll be at a movie when
you get home"—and sounded piqued when Asa came to the
phone. It would have been better to catch him out, drinking
illegally in Central Square, busy on a sofa with a girl whose
parents weren't home. He was there. It was irrefutable. But
what was he doing?

Asa biked back down Brattle through the puddles for a third
time, accompanied by a thick slice of yellow moon. The trees
leaned toward him, waving their soft leaves. It was a gauntlet
he had to run. Seductive patches of gold windows held scenes

of family life. Above, the sky was gashed by every color in the long, straight lines of summer sunset. He was headed for the intersection of five streets, a pentacle as potent as one drawn in chalk on a tiled floor in sixteenth-century Spain.

Overseeing this junction, but set back behind a wrought-iron fence and a stand of Colonial elms, was the Solas' house. Fourteen black-framed windows dared a passerby to look in, but there was nothing to see. It was a most ungiving façade, entirely folded in upon itself; a hundred windows wouldn't have changed that. Boxwood hedges crept up on it; wisteria as knotted as beech-tree roots veiled the porch that extended the length of the front. Someone, though not, surely, Professor Sola, had planted daylilies below the box, and their wrinkled orange heads fell on the lawn at dusk like falling stars. Hanging over everything was the rigorous unavailability of the house. It was absolutely a façade, because nothing could be like it. There was the echoing vacancy of a stage set: a twinkle of secrets from a light in a third-story room; a trill of curtains moving as a body made a breeze passing the long windows in front.

Asa slid his old black Raleigh behind the rhododendrons that flanked the door. It was his spot. Reuben's Peugeot, as young as the summer, leaned against a laurel bush now past blooming. Further down the drive two other bikes sprawled on the gravel. These belonged to Parker, a classmate of Asa's at Choate, and Roberto, Reuben's older brother. Asa, with the care that comes of relative poverty, checked that no glint of metal showed through the gloss of leaves, then rang the doorbell.

He felt the lightening of his blood that followed the far-off, clocklike dongs of the bell. He was sixteen, and for the first time he loved someone. New muscles in his arms quivered, his back became alert, and his stomach pushed against his diaphragm, nauseating him slightly with anticipation. He wondered who would answer the bell. It was Roberto.

"We're upstairs," he said, and turned down the hall, leaving Asa to shut the door. From the back he resembled Reuben. They shared a beautiful posture, womanly in its grace and length. Asa followed him up the back stairs. On the second floor Roberto began to whistle. This annoyed Asa, but he knew it was to cover their footsteps for the father who was behind one of the twelve closed doors that ringed the stairs. Roberto whistled constantly, breathily, to interject himself into events, to protest his position. Suddenly he stopped and turned his fox face over his shoulder.

"Did you get them?"

"Not yet. I have to wait for the weekend, when my father brings his bag home."

"Doesn't he keep a cabinet? I thought doctors kept cabinets of emergency medicine at home."

"It's locked."

"Break in."

That was it, thought Asa, that was the difference, the reason he felt himself always lacking and yearning. They lived in a simple universe. Their desires dictated their actions, so that their lives had the quality of purity, unreflection, unswerving faithfulness—to themselves. He had lived so long for responsibility, consideration, and compromise that beside the Solas he felt polluted and deflected. For whose pleasure was his life? Roberto's tapered hand opened the door. Haziness from cigarettes and young sweat interfered with the view. But Asa could see some bare legs and the beaming box of the television. This door Roberto was willing to close, and as he did, the gust of cooler, clearer air from the hall lifted the atmosphere a little, revealing a bed, with an obscured occupant, and the torso belonging to the legs, which were kneeling in front of the television. It was Parker, fiddling with the dials, wearing white boxer shorts and a waterproof Rolex on an alligator (and not waterproof) band. Asa thought the alligator ostentatious; he sported a flat gold pocket watch when dressed for school and not, as now, dressed in farm-faded denim and a T-shirt. His eyes were adjusting; the bed rumbled and he saw Reuben rise from the foaming white of the sheets, naked, a cigarette between his thin, pale lips.

"Hey, baby," Reuben said.

Tracks of ice ran down Asa's back and he turned from Reuben to the television. Unwatched, but knowing himself perceived, Reuben stretched his arms above his head and arched himself toward the ceiling. All four boys had the same coloring, but what was healthy, pink, and blond on Asa and Parker, and somewhat sallow on Roberto, on Reuben burned white and terrifying in clarity. His hair crested back in a triangle from his forehead in near-silver streaks. All the skin of his body, as Asa could plainly see were he to leave off watching a policeman chase a crook, was a pearly unmarked acreage stretched tight against his veins, which showed their purple mileage. His muscles and bones were prominent and his limbs were monkeylike, active and inquisitive-looking. This was especially true of his feet. Pointing to his left toe, his penis, pale and thin, lay with authority against his body. He was not naked, but a nude; in this he was different from his friends. They were unformed and uneasy enough to feel themselves exposed when stripped. He was finished, per-fected, and above all, pleased.

"Get dressed, Sola," said Parker, the only one brave enough to express their common embarrassment. "Get your pants on." Turning to Asa, who sat dumbly staring at the screen, he asked, "Did you get them?"

"Jesus, why don't you say hello first? Roberto asked me

the same thing. When I've got them, I'll give them to you."

"We want them," said Reuben, "so get them." He had put on his pants.

"I'll get them. I'll get them. Leave me alone." But Asa was reluctant to get them and furious that they caught his reluctance. "I have to wait for the weekend, when Father brings his bag home, and then I have to wait for them to go out to dinner or something. But I'll get them."

Nobody said anything. Everybody looked at Asa. Reuben took the situation in hand. "Let's swim," he said, and opened the door.

It was beyond midsummer; the crickets made a wonderful racket in counterpoint with the plosh of the pool's water. Parker dove in straight and vanished without bubbles, still wearing his boxers. Roberto began to skim the surface of the pool with a long-handled net and to whistle. Reuben took his pants off again and draped himself at the shallow end, his toes curling and uncurling around the water. Parker's sleeked head, almost white in the queer luminescence of July (stars, lights they'd left burning on the third floor, the pink blur of Boston smeared on the southern rim of the sky), came up near Reuben's feet. Roberto stood beside Reuben, armed with his net.

But Asa lingered on the flagstones, watching his friends. The night had pressed up to them and to him, confusing their shapes. They seemed to have lost their faces and become statues. Even, thought Asa, they were momentarily manifest gods. Reuben sat with a leg drawn up to his chest, his hands linked across the knee; Parker and Roberto flanked him like guards. Parker had leaned his head on Reuben's calf to steady himself in the water. Their eyes, in the dark, were also dark. Asa had a sharp understanding of the future—that is, a time when *this* would be the past. Time was rushing through and around him, he almost heard it whistling, and this awareness rounded the world somehow and made it sweet. Everything had a sweetness, a momentariness that captivated; behind him the rose trellis hummed with bees who were now asleep but would be there buzzing in the morning and so buzzed now. The circularity of things! He was safe in time, he was slung in a mesh of inevitability. And then his feeling of safety began to ebb. The whistle got sharper, almost hurt; it was a disinterested, determined sound, not made for his delight but the byproduct of gears as big as galaxies that turned for their own satisfaction. He—all of them—could be flung up anywhere, beached at misery, repetition, early death. The trio at the edge of the water was still fixed, as though they knew themselves to be well posed, but the glow of the perceived moment was gone; now they looked stuck. Nothing will stay the same, thought Asa, and this sad, simple idea calmed him. It returned him, somewhat battered, to his knowledge of the perishability of the present. He wanted to be rid of the whistling, the largeness. The present, with the promise of six more weeks of itself (the pool, the party Reuben would give on Saturday night, the twelve dollars he would pocket on Friday), was firm ground. He landed with relief.

On Friday night Parker turned up for dinner at the Thayers'. He was a cousin—his mother, Emily Graves, now Whiting, was the younger sister of Uncle John's wife. "Not a blood cousin," Asa's mother had muttered at ten-thirty on another evening after Parker had shown up unexpectedly and eagerly eaten seconds. "Julia, what difference does it make? Ten generations ago we were all William the Conqueror," Dr. Thayer said. "Robert, Robert," said the mother. Asa loved his father in these moods. Too often he behaved as though he were himself William. "This family thing can be carried too far," he said to Asa, who had planted himself in a chair hoping his father would continue. "It cannot," said Julia Thayer. "In the end, everyone except the family is a stranger."

"What's wrong with strangers?" asked Asa. His parents turned toward him. His father coughed. "They don't understand," said his mother.

"Pure xenophobia," said Asa to the mirror at midnight. It was a word he had learned recently. "I suppose I am to marry a cousin as well, a third or fourth cousin so as not to be inbred." He thought of the Solas, who were not even the same race—whatever that was—and the girls who appeared at their house on weekends, who had long white necks, pressed linen shorts, no curfews. Some of them were cousins of his, probably; some of them were not at all, not possibly.

So, Friday night, the night before the party at the Solas', Parker sat with the Thayers in the dark dining room with mauve walls and red-purple wood furniture, and ate six thin slices of roast beef, five boiled potatoes, and a few string beans. Both he and Asa drank milk from cobalt glasses; the Thayers drank a fair red wine. For dessert there was pound cake and strawberries. Dr. Thayer ate white grapes, his passion. He never shared them. They were placed before him by his wife every evening, in a small cut-glass bowl rimmed with silver.

"How's school, boys?" he asked, between grapes. Asa and Parker didn't say anything. "Harvard or Yale?" persisted Dr. Thayer.

"Oh, Harvard for sure," said Parker. He kicked Asa gently under the table.

"I don't know yet," said Asa. "We don't have to decide until November. Maybe I'll go to Princeton, Dad." He had no desire to go to Princeton.

"Playboys."

"No, sir, it's really become a serious school." Parker, earnest and confidential, leaned toward Asa's father. Asa hated this transformation of his friend and dreaded the cynical post-conversation comments he would hear as they biked to the Solas' later. "I think Asa might really enjoy himself there. Very good English literature courses there—"

"Not your interest," Dr. Thayer said. He did not meet Asa's eyes. "Southern atmosphere, not conducive to study."

"Much too far away," put in Asa's mother.

"It's just a thought," said Asa.

"Parker, do have some more cake. I'm afraid we seem to have finished the strawberries."

The Thayers were going to a piano recital given by a niece of Dr. Thayer's, at Paine Hall. Julia Thayer stood in front of the hall mirror patting her hair while Parker downed his cake. "You'll clear, won't you, dear," she commanded, lifting her voice into the dining room. "Robert." Dr. Thayer rose. Grape stems wiggled on the damask in front of his place.

"Going swimming, boys?" He sounded hopeless; Asa felt a surge of strength. He would go to Princeton, he would go swimming, he would marry a Phoenician.

"It's a hot night," said Parker.

"Give my love to Lilly," Asa said. He did like Lilly, the pianist. She hadn't gone to college at all, nor married, and lived in a bit of a slum near the river.

"You ought to have come," said his mother, "but it *is* a hot night. It must be lovely," she went on, turning to her husband, "to have a pool." He wasn't paying attention to her; he was putting his black bag into the coat closet, on the shelf next to the hats.

"Ah, Friday," he sighed. "Summer. Let's go over to the island next weekend, Julia?"

"We've got the Whitings for dinner Saturday. Not yours," she called hastily to Parker. "Your Uncle Johnny."

"Who gives a damn?" Parker muttered into his cake.

They left. Beyond the curtains the sky was pale, pale blue and changing. The boys sprawled in their chairs, silent, hot. Asa rummaged through the stems, looking for just one grape. None. The crickets began to whir, then stopped. The clock in the hall clicked into place and boomed the half hour. Parker poured himself a glass of wine. Asa, nervous, wanting to protect the remaining food, cleared the table.

"Do you always do what they tell you?"

"What else is there to do?" Asa held the roast on its silver platter in one hand and a clutch of linen napkins in the other. "I'm not here most of the time. I hate arguing with them. They're so"—his eyes shut—"sort of dead, you know? They just go dead. It makes me feel awful. Hell with them. I clear the table, they don't tell me when to come home."

"But they do. You say they do."

"Yes, but they don't mean it."

"Don't mean it," repeated Parker. He drank some wine.

"It's a reflex, I think."

"Let's get them now." Parker looked around for more wine, but Asa had taken it. "Do you know where the bag is?"

"In the coat closet." Asa didn't want to do it, he didn't want to have anything to do with it, but Parker was staring at him like a conscience—a bad conscience—and he was trapped. "Let's forget it," he said, brave for an instant.

"Come on, chickenshit. Come on."

Asa went to the hall, lifted the bag down, and slammed it onto the table. Then he turned his face. Parker opened it. Inside a stethoscope glittered, bottles jingled against each other, bright, full of colors. There were also a pipe, an extra pair of glasses, an Agatha Christie novel, a bone-handled brush. Asa felt sad to see his father's mute possessions strewn on the tablecloth. Parker rummaged with determination.

"Hey," he said, "codeine." He pocketed a brown bottle.

"No, you said just the amyl nitrite."

"Come on." Parker didn't stop poking through the pockets. "There." He held up a small glass vial winking a flicker of violent yellow. "That's one."

"I don't know if there are any more."

"Sure there are. We need at least four, one for each of us. Or don't you want any?"

Asa said nothing. Parker seemed to be taking hours finding them. Asa heard the ghost of his parents' car in the driveway, the door opening. The clock boomed again. Eight-fifteen. Parker had found another ampule.

"You have to leave some," said Asa. "He'll be suspicious. See how many there are and leave at least half."

"Suppose there are only two? Nah, I'll take them. He'll decide he's getting old and forgot when he used them."

Asa knew his father would never decide that. In truth, he saw no way to avoid a scene in which his father, pale and clenched, accused him of stealing. The only way would be if the whole bag vanished, as in a robbery. Silver, portraits, black bag—he wondered if they could arrange it. Leave the door unlocked. Then he'd be careless, reprehensible, but not a thief. That seemed too elaborate, and so calculating as to make him guiltier. Asa blanked his mind out and waited for Parker to finish. The bag was full of treasures, and Parker wanted them all.

"What's this—phenobarbital. We could really get high on this. This is terrific. And here's some, some—"

"It's aspirin, for God's sake. Just hurry up. Just get the ampules and let's go."

"You are chickenshit." Parker's face was too even-featured to express much emotion; his face appeared every year in the school catalogue, poring over a book in the sunlit library. "Building young men of character . . ." To compensate he had developed a gravelly, rather ominous voice. "I bet you're not even going to try it."

"I don't have to try it."

"Because you know what it's like? You've never tried it. You're just scared."

"So what," said Asa. "Let's go." He took the bag and put it back on its perch. He wanted to ride off on his bicycle to New Hampshire and disappear into the woods.

Instead the two of them rode down Brattle Street away from the sunset. Asa had left the back door unlocked in case he decided to stage a burglary in the middle of the night. Parker's pockets jingled. The street flashed below their tires; they moved as fast as airplanes through the humid night. At the intersection in front of the Solas' they stopped, Parker jamming his brakes hard enough to skid himself around facing Asa.

Somnolent evening in July, the crickets, the first patches of light in windows, Parker's form dense against the approaching dark—Asa saw all this, all this crept toward him oppressively. He swallowed, blinked, tried to clear his head out. But his head was as full as if he had a flu. "I'm off," he said, and rode away, down Brattle Street past the long curved driveway that drew Parker in like an arm.

It was Friday and he had money, so he went to Harvard Square. He ate a hot-fudge sundae at Schrafft's. He went to the Out-of-Town News and leafed through *Look* until he was told to "buy it or put it away." He put it away. There was nothing left to do except try to sneak into the movie at the

Brattle Theatre or stand in front of the entrance to the Casablanca, the bar under the theatre, and hope some seniors from Andover or Choate would appear and take him in. He was not in the mood for a solo confrontation with the bartender about his age; groups were less likely to be harassed and more likely to cajole the bartender into serving a few beers.

For fifteen minutes he stood at the door to the Casablanca, a sorry figure with his hands pushed all the way in to the pockets of his pressed khakis. He had a sense of himself looking forlorn and ungainly and had just determined to leave—to bike to Walden Pond for a midnight swim—when Parker's older brother, Clem, appeared with a girl. Clem was a junior at Harvard; the girl looked to be Asa's age. She was lanky and dressed in red, and she had a wide-jawed face. Her full skirt swung out, then wrapped itself around her thighs as, twirled by Clem, she turned to greet Asa.

"Hey, meeting the boys?" asked Clem. He held the girl close with a heavy arm. He was a lacrosse star; his nose had been broken twice before his senior year at Choate. "Oh yeah, you're not of age." Clem moved his hand from the girl's waist to her neck, so her bare skin shone between his broad fingers. "Come on in, we'll buy you a drink."

"Great," said Asa. He extended his hand. "Asa Thayer."

"Oh, this is Jo," said Clem. He opened the double doors and pushed her in before she and Asa could touch. "My cousin," he added, over his shoulder. He winked.

"First cousin?" asked Asa, when they were seated.

"Third," said Jo. She had large teeth, very white and well tended, and a rough, low voice like Parker's. She took a package of Luckys from her red skirt and put one in her mouth. Asa, who had no matches, looked at Clem, but Clem was ordering drinks. "Hey," growled Jo, and she put her hand on Clem's arm. The cigarette dangled from her lip. "Hey, light me."

They had vodka martinis and Asa got drunk. It happened suddenly, in the middle of his second drink. A film of pleasure softened the contours of the bar and the two faces opposite him, giving everything a promising glisten. He felt hopeful; Jo leaned her head toward him when she talked, which she did more and more as Clem settled into his third martini. She talked about her hockey team at Winsor, about the sailing she was hoping to do over Labor Day, about her sister Anne's new spaniel—"he loves to go out on the boat with us"—and the Pontiac she'd been promised for graduation. Clem leaned back and didn't listen, but looked at her pale throat, which vibrated in the dark. She never asked a question, although her speech was dotted with interrogatives: "Do you see what I'm talking about?" "Isn't that a sketch?" "Don't you agree?" She tossed these first at Clem, then at Asa, snapping her wide, wicked eyes from one boy to the other. She was wicked, Asa saw through his haze, she was wickedly, deeply full of her flesh and her lanky limbs and her raspy, monotonous voice. There was an untidiness about her—a spot on her skirt, grit under her nails—that gave Asa an erotic tingle. She was not, quite, a girl he could imagine taking to a dinner dance. Undoubtedly she was taken to them, but he knew she would be the only one of her kind there.

So they drifted through their third drink, Clem watching Jo, Asa interjecting ums and reallys, which were hardly needed. It was ten o'clock and the bar was starting to fill up. It was an odd bar, serving three distinct groups who segregated themselves automatically. Hard-drinking lawyers in their thirties with no reason to go home sat at the bar itself, in low conversation with the whiskey-colored bartender. Harvard boys and their dates sat in the wicker booths that lined three walls. In the middle, at wobbling tables meant for two, quartets of homosexual men spilled their stingers on the checked tablecloths. These groups were not absolute—doctors, writers, and professors joined the lawyers at the stools; the homosexuals included women with brightly colored stockings who were not homosexual; and prep-school boys toting finishing-school girls passed themselves off as their older brothers and sisters along the wall. Still, as in all bars, sorrow, sex, and love were the preoccupations, and a man hoping to swamp his sadness in gin doesn't talk to a man thinking to score, or thinking of how those cashmere shoulders will look at forty. The only overlap occurred when one of the younger boys caught the eye of a man in the middle. Asa and Reuben and Parker had drawn many unacknowledged glances on other nights. Only Reuben had noticed them; when he pointed out admirers ("That fellow in the yellow shirt, he's sweet for you, Asa") the others cringed. "Knock it off," Parker would say. "Fresh flesh," Reuben said, pinching Asa's thigh, which hung over the arm of his chair. He alerted them to this other world, this distorted mirror world, and to their own power in it. "For a little handjob you could get a Peugeot ten-speed." "Yucchh," said Parker. He spoke for them all, despite Reuben's bravado. They bent their blond heads over their beers and the man in the yellow shirt sighed. "Like a young lion," he said to his stinger and his three companions, seeing in his drink Asa's lips open from sleepiness and the pale beard he didn't need to shave.

Asa, sixteen, having kissed two nice girls, one at a dinner dance only two months before (Jenny, dark-haired, tasting of a cigarette sneaked and shared behind a rosebush), having secretly, in June, spent most of his paycheck on a whore fifteen years older, who took a phone call in the middle of his session and whose thick waist he gripped with sad passion, having nobody to imagine her as, was looking—staring—at Jo and thinking of—longing for—Reuben and company. He missed the comfort of being understood. He missed the familiar shape and smell of Reuben, and the dizzying competition among the other three for Reuben's admiration, which, though hard to provoke, could be lavish. So when Jo, talked out at ten-fifteen, asked the first question of the evening, "What are you doing with your summer?," he answered immediately, "Hanging out at the Solas'."

"Reuben Sola? Those rich Jews over near Sparks Street?"

"Yes," Asa said, startled, "them." It was a new outlook on the situation.

"Oh, well. Why don't you come out on the boat next week? I think we're all going to sail up from my uncle's place in Duxbury to Manchester. Clem's coming, isn't that right?" Clem didn't nod. "I think Parker's coming too—you're classmates, aren't you? I'm sure he's planning to come. And I'd love you to come." She took another cigarette from her pack and kept her eyes on Asa. "It'll be grand, don't you think?"

"I'm working."

"Oh. I didn't know you had a job. You didn't say you had a job."

"Yes, I'm working," repeated Asa, taking refuge behind the gas pump and the hot, black tarmac. "Thanks, though. Maybe next year." Then, sensing she must be placated more, "It sounds like it will be fun."

"They're not so bad," said Clem suddenly. "He's an interesting man, Sola. Got a great art collection—you know that's a Goya he's got in the living room. Got some terrific dirty etchings, too, some Picassos. And a Daumier. You know that Daumier in the library?"

"Clemmy, I didn't know you knew about art. Isn't that a sketch? Where in the world did he get that stuff?"

"My minor concentration. Major concentration, European history; minor in art. Get the whole picture. I don't know where he got it. Paris, I suppose. He was in France during the war."

"I think I'm going to major in English," Asa said.

"Oh, are you going to be a beatnik?" Jo put her hands in her red skirt and flipped the hem around her knees. "Live in a garret and stuff?" She was nasty from too many martinis.

"I didn't know you knew the Solas," said Asa.

"A girl in my class went out with Reuben last fall. I think it was Reuben. He's the younger one, right? The good-looking one? Who doesn't look Jewish."

But Asa had been talking to Clem. Clem was gone again, thinking of the whole picture, or Jo's legs, or whether to have a fourth martini. "He did," said Asa. "Who was that?" Everything was getting far away from him.

"Marjorie Fish. She has curly hair."

"Oh yes, Marjorie," Asa said. It was news to him. The evening was full of news, which he wanted to be considering, alone.

Some social situations are difficult to disengage from, especially at sixteen. There was the matter of the bill (Asa refused to let Clem pay for his drinks), and snagging the waitress, and waiting for the change from Asa's end-of-the-week five. Then there was a round of invitations to sail, swim, come to Western art classes at Harvard, buy gas at Asa's station—none of which any of them wanted to do. Asa wanted air.

"Well, well—" He had managed to stand up. "Good night." Their smoky faces looked up at him; both had petulant expressions, and he realized they wanted to be alone as much as he did. He fairly ran out the door.

There was his bicycle leaning on a lamppost, the dew of

the hot night streaked down the street, the quietness everywhere. It was ten-forty. Asa turned his wheels west and rode
down Brattle Street until he came to the Solas' house. Then
he stood on the street and looked at it.

He was trying to impose his new information onto the
familiar shape. He wanted to see it as a Jewish palace, a folly
full of plundered goods, because that was how he understood
Jo's remarks. He thought of the paintings—those Goyas and
Daumiers he had ignored, imagining them some Jewish
equivalent of the ancestors who lived on his stairway—and
the black statuettes in the bookshelves (these were by Degas,
Clem had said), and tried to see them as objects with their
own importance; that was how he defined art. They stead-
fastly remained Professor Sola's things, the way his mother's
blue-and-white ginger jar on the mantelpiece was hers by
virtue of the pencils it had held since the beginning of time.
He didn't understand the indignation in Jo's voice. She had
made it sound as though the Solas had no right to these things
or this house, with its beautiful arced driveway, its pre-Rev-
olutionary trees. But for Asa the Solas had merged with their
house just as all the owners of Brattle Street houses had; if
they had accomplished it in fifteen years rather than a century,
that was to their credit.

There were lights on the third floor. They were up there,
Parker and Roberto, Reuben was up there, they had beer,
they had drugs that had made them first dizzy, then sick,
now bored and waiting for the next event. In the Casablanca
Clem was breathing martinis into Jo's small and not-clean
ear, the bartender was wiping the copper counter, the clock
above the bar was clicking on its electric way toward midnight. Asa was standing on the street straddling his old Raleigh while the night cooled. All his options were the opposite—
constrictions. Back in Harvard Square there was nothing ex-

cept circling around the empty, gray streets, leaving tire marks in the dew. At home just the ill-fitting tread on the second step on the way upstairs, the awful square bottle of milk, blue as ice, from whose thick, cream-clotted lip he would drink while holding the refrigerator open with his left hand and staring blankly at the leftovers in their covered bowls. And here, upstairs behind the canvas shade that smelled like second grade because it smelled of paste and dust and sunshine, Reuben lolling on the braided carpet, satisfied without Asa. Nobody was looking out the window for him; nobody was out on bicycles following his trail.

He could go in by the secret way—through a door in the basement, where Reuben kept a mattress to sleep on, and kiss girls on, when he was supposed to be somewhere else. For instance, at Andover. Reuben took the train back to Cambridge on wintry Thursdays and lay there, under his father's feet, reading magazines, watching the day go away through the slits of glass near the ceiling. Then in the dark down to North Station, onto the six o'clock train, back in the dorm by seven. Asa knew how to get in, but he didn't want to get in. He wanted, he realized, to stand on the street and be forlorn.

Asa made a short, difficult foray into his mind to look for the source of his wish to be forlorn and didn't find it there. What's the matter with me? was the deepest he could penetrate. His heart, calling for attention, made a little flurry of beats, but he put that down to martinis. He tried again: What's the matter with you? By removing himself this one step more he kept himself safe from knowing.

He rode home and drank milk and went to bed.

Everything was different in the morning. First, it was wonderfully hot. At eight-thirty the tarmac at the gas station was oozing under his sneakers. Heat, Asa had noticed, exhausted adults; the party at the Solas' would be less chaperoned than usual. Professor Sola would sit near his air conditioner and look at his bronzes rather than pace his flagstone terrace with a glass of gin the way he tended to do when Reuben gave parties. Second, his parents had not noticed the unlocked door, and his father had taken his black bag out of the closet, opened it, put his lunch into it, and gone off to his half-day at the office (lunch on the riverbank in front of the hospital as always) without finding anything amiss.

And then, in the middle of the morning, Jo appeared in a Buick, wearing a sleeveless green blouse that made her eyes, which last night had been yellow, green also. She put her elbow on the edge of the door, exposing her pale armpit, and rasped out, "Asa." Asa was stacking cans of oil. The day was so hot his hands ached from touching the seething metal. And Jo looked cool like fruit—all fresh white skin and green cloth peeping out her window.

"I thought you were going sailing," said Asa, standing up. He finished his pyramid of cans and went, automatically, toward her gas tank.

"Hey, I don't want gas," Jo said. She moved across the seat and leaned out the other window, where Asa was pointing the nozzle at her. "I wanted to see you."

A few drops of gas dripped from the tip of the hose. "You did?" He put the pump line back in its socket. "I thought you were going sailing." He realized he'd already said this and blushed.

Jo, watching Asa blush, lifted her arms to her hair and pushed her hands into it, pulling it straight back from her face. She had thick hair, probably close to brown in the winter, but now tawny and shiny from the sun. She let her hands fall down abruptly. "Hot," she said. "Want to get some iced tea?"

"I don't get lunch until eleven-thirty."

"I'll come back." She drove out cautiously. This surprised Asa; he had imagined her a reckless driver. She flashed her taillights at him as she left the lot. He had an hour to fill.

First, time was slow and the sun made a glare in the spilled gasoline. Then two people wanted oil. When Jo came back there was a line of six cars waiting for gas, and Asa was sprinting from window to window taking money and orders. Jo parked near the office and smoked a Lucky. Asa did not look up, did not watch her smoke making circles on the solid atmosphere, counted change instead, said, "Thank you, sir," kept her a secret from himself for a few minutes. Then he was done, and had to face her and where to have lunch in the nether end of Cambridge where nobody either of them knew lived or ate.

"Wait a minute," he mumbled as he passed her on his way to wash. His face in the mirror was tracked with grit. His hands smelled of fuel, and then of fuel and yellow soap. Through the open vent above the sink he heard the scratch of her match lighting her second cigarette. He was keeping her waiting, which was ungentlemanly.

But what was he to do with her? There was a sub shop down the block; he imagined Jo in a red booth with her elbow avoiding a puddle of Coke. He preferred imagining her in the gloom of the Casablanca. He stood on tiptoe and looked at her through the vent. He had three dollars and she looked like a five-dollar lunch, maybe even an eight-dollar lunch. She was putting on pink lipstick, which didn't become her. She had a mirror that fit the palm of her hand; she held it two feet away with an extended arm so as to get the whole picture. Her self-absorption enchanted Asa. He was spying on her privacy, which added interest to an already interesting scene. Jo and her mirror did a duet they'd practiced many times: She turned her head left and right, checking the sweep of her hair against her pale cheeks; she pushed her nose close to the glass and examined her pores—were they bigger? Did she need to use some alcohol?—then drew back and smiled; this showed her teeth, and she licked them quickly to make them shine. The mirror obediently reflected the prettiest girl in the parking lot. Asa's arches began to ache from standing on tiptoe. Jo put her mirror in her purse and pulled out another cigarette.

"Hey, Thayer," she said suddenly, in a normal tone of voice, as though he were standing beside her. Asa dashed from the washroom, pulling from his pocket the matches he had found that morning after a long search through the shelves of oil filters, spark plugs, wrenches, and gray rags. When he reached her she had lighted her cigarette.

"Let's eat," he said. He hoped if he said it firmly a pleasant sandwich shop would spring up on the sidewalk around the corner. But in the end they took a red booth and waited for their grinders (Asa's meatball, Jo's Italian cold cuts with everything) to arrive.

It was a $1.70 lunch, $2.10 with two iced teas and tip. Jo's paper plate glistened with fallen chips of onion and green pepper. Asa was fearful of getting tomato sauce on his face.

"How come you didn't go sailing this weekend?" Asa ventured, after a few difficult bites of meatball.

"God, you don't forget a thing, do you?" said Jo. She folded a thick slice of salami in half and popped it in her mouth. A trickle of oil was left on her chin. "I thought it would be more fun to go to the party."

"Reuben's party?"

"Yes. Is there another one?"

"I don't think so." As other parties would not be worth going to, he hadn't listened for news of them. "Have you ever been to one?"

"A Sola party? No, but I've heard about them. I've heard people end up swimming with nothing on and, well, absolute orgies."

Asa had never been at an orgy; had he been uninvited? "Not quite orgies," he said, "but it gets pretty wild." It hadn't. The pleasure lay in the space—the pool, the long, lovely lawn, the knowledge that Professor Sola could patrol only one area at a time, the idea of possible wildness.

"Clemmy's going to take me." Having announced this, Jo filled herself up with a large installment of cold cuts. Asa was disappointed; he had reckoned on asking her to go with him— offering himself as her escort. It occurred to him that she was tormenting him, and he wondered why she had turned up. Surely not just to bother him. If he'd been twenty he might have had the wit to say, "I'm so delighted you came to have lunch with me," and watched her face for clues, but all he could think of was the way she might taste, if he were able to lean across the Formica and put his mouth on hers. Or her cheek, or the bone near her eye, where her lashes made a shadow trellis.

"Tell me about Reuben," Jo said.

"Why do you want to know about him?"

"He seems interesting. All you boys hang around with him—he must be interesting. Tell me some things about him."

"All who?" asked Asa, postponing. "Just me and Parker."

"Oh, Clem goes over there, doesn't he? And I know some

other people . . ." But she wasn't going to say who. She looked at Asa as if the information he wasn't giving out were a match he wasn't striking for her cigarette.

"He's not very good at school," said Asa. "He's at Andover, you know, and he was on academic probation all last year. I don't think he studies. He's very smart."

"How do you know he's smart?"

"Well, you just know."

"And you are good at school?" Jo put her elbows on the back of the booth, so her shirt pressed against her breasts and her collarbone made a half-circle of white against her skin.

"No, but I'm better than he is. He doesn't even write papers—at least he says he only writes the papers that interest him."

"What interests him?"

"He likes dissecting things. Frogs."

"Ugh!" Jo put her arms down and held hands with herself.

"And he likes American history. He says it's a string of disasters and it cheers him up."

"Huh? I don't get it. What's he *like,* I mean, what's it like to be with him?"

"It's fun," said Asa. "He's always thinking of something new to do."

"What kinds of things?"

"Why don't you talk to him yourself?"

"Jealous?" She smiled. "I've heard that he climbs things. Buildings. Is that true?"

"Oh." Asa didn't know what to say, because it was a secret. Reuben had a policy of climbing the scaffolding of every building under construction in Cambridge. There were not many of these, and they were usually lower than six stories, but in June a ten-story apartment was going up in North Cambridge and he had, in the middle of the night, scaled it alone, lighted only by the beams from passing cars and the hissing street lamp forty feet away. At least he claimed to have done this. He made them promise to keep it a secret. "Next time," he'd said to Parker and Asa, "you'll come along. It's wonderful up at the top. They're going to build something around the corner from this apartment building—I saw them digging up the ground. Let's hope it's fifteen stories." Asa hoped it wouldn't be.

"Where did you get that idea?" he asked her.

Jo smiled again. "You know he's very rich. I mean, he's got his own money, and when he's twenty-one he'll have more. Not rich the way you and I are—"

Are we? thought Asa.

"—but like movie stars. He's sixteen, isn't he?"

"Yes. But he'll be seventeen next week. This is an advance birthday party. His birthday's on Tuesday."

"You watch, he'll buy a car on his birthday. His own— you see? I can't do that. My parents will give me a car, but I don't have my own money to get one."

"What sort of a car?" Asa thought of a wonderful car, a tapered, bottle-green Chevy with the softest backseat in the Northeast, long enough to stretch Jo out on while he skillfully undid the buttons of her blouse.

"And because they're Jews," Jo continued, "he'll get the fanciest car he can find."

"Why? Why does that mean . . ." He put his finger in the cooling puddle of tomato sauce on his plate and drew a circle in it.

"Oh you! You don't understand anything!" Jo laughed at him, and it was not a pleasant laugh. "We're cousins, aren't we? Aren't you and Clemmy cousins?"

"Not first cousins. Second, I think."

"And I'm Clemmy's cousin—"

"He said third. That's barely cousins. That means we're fifth cousins."

"Well, *you* know what I mean. We're related."

"So what?" said Asa. He stared at her eyes, which were yellow again. "Does that mean I can't kiss you?" He blushed. Jo, however, did not blush.

"Try it," she said. It was a dare.

"I have to get back to work," said Asa, and he made a pile of nickels on the table.

"You are a responsible little fellow."

"How old are you?" Asa was standing up, and angry. "You're my age, aren't you?"

"Sure," said Jo. "Or maybe just a bit younger. It's good for the girl to be younger, isn't it?"

Then she stood up as well, and came near him, so he could smell her and feel the warmth of her limbs. She smelled of onions and smoke. He moved away. "I'm late," he said. "I'm sorry, I must get back."

"I'm coming, stop rushing me."

Walking down the block to the gas station they were silent. Asa's hand brushed hers for a second, but she neither flinched nor turned her palm toward his. The air smelled of hot rubber and gasoline. The night to come, which earlier had seemed a chilly-blue oasis—the water in the pool, the music soaring out of the speakers that hung off the garage, the fellowship of himself and Reuben and Parker contrasted with the dozens of strangers in whose company, bolstered by his friends, he would be at ease—now might be as steamy and restless and incomprehensible as the day, all because of Jo.

"So you're coming tonight," he asked, as she got into her car.

"Oh yes," she said. She looked at herself in the rearview

mirror and blew herself, or maybe him, a kiss. "I'll be there, looking great."

"Okay," said Asa. Okay, what? he asked himself. Okay, she can look great? Okay, she can come tonight? He wished that she would break her arm playing tennis or that Clem would whisk her off to a fancy restaurant in Boston where they wouldn't eat dinner until ten. He wanted—was it privacy with Reuben? Perhaps relief from her attractiveness. "See you later, then."

She left, in her slow, deliberate way, and gave a honk as she turned the corner.

At ten o'clock the party was rising to its crest. The fifty or so guests had passed through the stages of entry, huddling with three friends, scouting the crowd for romance, and dancing with unknowns, and had started to form a mass, a crowd with its own mood. It wasn't clear where the mood came from; it wasn't even clear what the mood was—but Asa felt the change. The mood existed independently of any particular person and had come over the moist patio like an ether, piped through the speakers with Chuck Berry. Asa felt turbulent, like a hurricane day in September, thick and changeable and poised on the edge of novelty. And he knew, from the faces around him, especially Roberto's, that everyone shared his sensations. Roberto's characteristic expression, which was petulance overlaid with a brash and false indifference, had shifted to anticipation. Girls who earlier had kept their dancing partners an arm's length away now pressed their cheeks on white broadcloth, leaving faint dabs of powder there at the end of the song. Boys who had arrived in ties (Asa had not) had pocketed them. Professor Sola had made his round, gin in hand, at nine-thirty, greeted Asa and Parker, whispered a few words to Reuben, and left. But before leaving he had done something that startled Asa into wondering about him. He was a tall bony man who usually wore a black suit, and he moved in an awkward, bony way, as if he consisted only of joints and cartilage. He scuffed along floors, so the boys always knew when he was coming. Tonight he had paused on his way back to the house and turned around, facing the lines of bobbing dancers, and stood watching for a while. Then he had walked, without scuffing, back to the edge of the pool and knelt, swiftly and easily, beside it. Folded up near the ground he looked to Asa more jagged and bloodless than usual. How odd, thought Asa, that Reuben is so unlike him. Professor Sola dipped his hand in the turquoise water and drew it toward him, cupped in his palm. The image of the simply colored paper lanterns strung above the terrace, pink and yellow, swayed on the surface of the pool. Again his hand slid through the water, and he swept his arm along with the ease that Reuben curled his arm to throw a ball. "Grace," he said. Then he did leave.

"Grace," repeated Asa. Was that a name or an idea? He couldn't decide which would be stranger. If a name, whose? And why was Professor Sola whispering it by the edge of the pool? Grace as an idea was something Asa associated with Bible studies, the story of the Good Samaritan, the drowsiness he felt after lunch, which was when the class was held. It was a puzzle.

Also puzzling was Jo, who hadn't arrived. Asa hunted down Parker, who was clasped in beige linen arms at the far corner of the terrace, and coughed.

"Hey, Parker," he said.

Parker lifted his head up and frowned. "I'm busy," he said, then turned the girl around and introduced her to Asa. She was about fifteen, her hair was the color of her dress, and her eyes were still shut, looking in at the memory of Parker's mouth. Her name was Amy.

"Sorry, but I wonder if your brother's coming."

"Clem? I don't know. Why should I know? Why don't you dance? He'll be here, if he's coming." Parker saw Asa wince at this string of rudeness and pulled a flask from his pocket. "Have a shot. Have a few shots and ask Lydia to dance."

"Who's Lydia?"

"There must be somebody here named Lydia. Find her and ask her to dance."

This was an assignment only Parker could have thought up or carried out. Asa couldn't go from girl to girl asking if her name was Lydia. Did Parker offer challenges like this just to make him, Asa, feel weak? He stomped into the garage, where Reuben had hidden beer in a cooler behind some snow tires, and stood in the gloom drinking. And in the gloom he saw something new in the garage: Reuben's car, predicted by Jo.

It was low, stout, white, and entirely novel to Asa. Its snub-nosed hood said PORSCHE. He walked around it once, looking at its handles and its single strip of chrome before peering through the glass to inspect the dashboard and seats. On the seats—red leather, bucket, ample—sat Reuben at the steering wheel and Jo on the right. His hand lay on her thigh; she was wearing the red skirt again. And her hand with its bitten nails grasped his wrist like a handcuff, as if it would never let go.

Asa stepped out of the garage into the pools of light cast by the paper lanterns on the driveway. His bicycle was leaning against a bush, and he wanted more than anything to be on it, riding down a dark country road without a thought for Reuben or any of them. No side street in all of Cambridge would do; he needed blackness, the hum and strum of a thousand animals poised at the edge of the woods watching him pass, the living, soft country night all around him, to erase what he wanted to erase. Therefore he walked back to the party.

Roberto sidled up to him and offered him a swig of something golden in a glass. Asa took it; it burned and stank like nothing he had ever drunk.

"What is that?" he asked. "Kerosene?"

"Special old brandy I stole from Papa. Where's Reuben?"

"Sitting in his car."

"All by himself?" When Asa didn't answer, Roberto asked again.

"No," said Asa after a while, "he's sitting with a girl."

Roberto did something unusual then. He put his arm around Asa's shoulders. They stood together, sharing the nasty brandy in silence. And because Roberto was making a special effort for him, Asa was comforted. At the same time he knew it was his sense of injury that let him accept Roberto; in the normal course of things Roberto was an extra, a cranky appendage he and Parker tolerated from loyalty to Reuben, who felt loyalty to his brother.

"We're both outsiders, aren't we," said Roberto suddenly. It wasn't a question. "I organized this damn party—all these parties, in fact. Did you know that? Reuben says, 'Let's have a party,' and then I call people up, I arrange for the beer, I spread the word around town, I even hang these stupid lanterns. But they look nice, don't they? I like the lanterns reflected in the pool. I do everything, and then I stand around watching it, while Reuben and Parker smooch with ninth graders in the bushes. I do attic patrol—you know what that is? Checking the upstairs bedrooms to make sure there aren't any couples in them. I even make sure Papa has a fresh drink every hour on my way downstairs from attic patrol."

"Why do you do it?"

"Oh, why not? I like a party too. Anyhow, it's what I do. Then I watch it. I watch people making fools of themselves, falling in the pool, getting lipstick on their cheeks, puking on a deck chair. I'm sort of the guardian of the party." He laughed and looked at Asa sideways. "And you're sort of the ghost of the party."

"What are you talking about?" Asa moved out from the shelter of Roberto's arm.

"You're never in the bushes smooching, you're always trailing around after them, jealous because they're smooching or they're drunker than you are and they're having more fun."

"The hell I am," said Asa. But Roberto wasn't listening to him.

"And you do what you have to do to pass—you know, to look as though you're part of the party. You dance a few rounds, and you carry a beer bottle, and you know enough not to arrive in a jacket and tie. But you're as out of it as I am. More. I live here, for Chrissake. I can tell everybody to go home. It's my house. Shall I do that? This isn't much of a party. The one in May was a lot better."

"No, oh, no," said Asa. Roberto, standing in the glare of his lanterns, seemed flooded with a sudden power, and Asa half believed that a snap of his fingers would cause the crowd to evaporate. But he also knew himself to be just suffering from the inconsistency of life: Jo was in the new car with Reuben, and he was a ghost, and he hadn't expected either of these events. So why shouldn't Roberto turn out to be a sorcerer? There was also the question of "Grace." Roberto had begun to whistle and tap his foot, signs that he was about to move away and make trouble elsewhere. "What was your mother's name?" asked Asa.

"We don't talk about her," Roberto said.

Asa knew that already. She was more unmentionable than the source of the Solas' money, which was variously reported, by Asa's parents, Parker, and Clem, to be from a drugstore chain, the Rothschilds (cousins, maybe?), or smuggled from Europe at the start of the war in the form of diamonds. Professor Sola's wife had been: blonde and bad—and this Asa knew from deduction.

Roberto was on the other side of the pool, jostling the dancers at the edge in the hope that some were unsteady enough to fall in. None did. Then he took up his skimming pole and cleaned the surface of the water, moving, with his net, the lanterns' garish daubs that like a new constellation ringed themselves in that liquid sky. He stirred the water and made little whirlpools and whistled and splashed. The long pole's end was interfering with Parker and Amy, who had come out of the shadows to dance. Roberto had managed to insert it between them, and every time he stirred, the pole described an unpredictable ellipse at the level of their knees.

"Pole," said Parker.

Roberto beat on, unheeding.

"Pole, you asshole!" Parker yelled. One moment later he grabbed the handle and flipped Roberto into the pool by jerking it from his hands. And then there was nothing to prevent everybody else from going in—the water was cool, dancing was hot, midnight had struck on the church clock up the street, and they were all young.

Asa, in his capacity of ghost, sat in a deck chair and waited to hear the car doors shut. He wanted a specific thing: Jo coming to him in the dark and kissing him. He imagined it with words—"Why are you sitting here in the dark? Why aren't you swimming?"—and without: her hands on his shoulders, her thigh pressing against his arm, which rested on the arm of the chair, the smell of her hair as it fell around his face; her two rather small lips pushing against his, tasting of lipstick and Luckys and her own secret taste, which would be peppermint; the instant when he pushed beyond her lips and into the heat of her mouth. Perhaps she would push her way into him first? The way her skirt would slip under his hands when he put them around her knees to hold her steady through their kiss. How they would, without having to walk or discuss it, be lying in grass hip to hip and be warm up and down from each other's heat. Her fingers undoing his buttons. Their shoes paired like sentries on the ground. A small pile of clothes, crickets singing to them, silk and silk, wet silk and dry of her stretched out for him.

When she did come, things happened so quickly he barely caught the details. She stood behind him, put one hand on his neck, and pulled his head backwards by his chin. She kissed him upside down, so he didn't know if her eyes were open or shut. It was a professional kiss; her tongue was in and out of him and the whole thing was over in ten seconds. She stood briefly behind him, still holding him on the shoulder, and they breathed together. Asa put his tongue between his lips to taste her again; she tasted, naturally enough, of Reuben—beery, yeasty, slightly tart from chlorine and sweat, a taste that, translated into smell, Asa could have identified anywhere.

"Do that again," he said, arching his neck back to her. His voice was low and thick, but he was pleading, not commanding. And Jo, with her excitable red skirt, was not a girl to be pleaded with. He knew that the instant the sentence was out. Overcoming centuries of inertia and miles of internal boundaries, Asa rose from his chair and turned around to embrace her. She wasn't there. He couldn't even see her disappearing into the garage.

He sat back in his chair. Was she now kissing Reuben, who was tasting Asa's taste in her? Or was she moving from Parker to Roberto to Harrison Grey, who always wore a seersucker suit to the party? Was she sitting next to Clem in his Ford while he pumped the gas pedal and hoped the car would start? If he waited for her again as intently as he had, would she reappear? He tried. This time he supplied himself with her breasts, whose dimensions he could guess from the moment when she had pressed herself against his shoulders, trying to reach the rims of his upper teeth with her tongue. But the taste, the Reuben-taste, which remained vivid in his mouth and mind, confused his image of her, so that her honey hair kept bleaching into Reuben's pale hair, and her small bony face, which looked, now that he thought of it, a little like Reuben's, kept looking exactly like Reuben's. Brandy and fury at being peripheral had him confused; a creature with a boy's face, breasts, and wearing something white—a ghost hermaphrodite—was what he had created for his fantasies. That sort of thing would never appear on the Solas' terrace to kiss him.

Beyond his outstretched feet the party sang the last verse of its song. The pool was empty and unruffled again. Those who had been in it were standing beside it with damp patches on their clothes saying good-bye to ones they had kissed or wished they'd kissed. Cars and bicycles were crunching the gravel of the driveway. The lanterns were pale, as though shining all evening had exhausted their pigment, and the table where ginger ale and orange juice (mixers for the vodka carried in silver flasks in back pockets) had been ranked like ninepins now held one bottle of beer with two cigarette butts in it. Roberto was sweeping up the broken glass surrounding the table by kicking it into a paper bag; the shards he trod on, exclaiming "Ping," as each one cracked. People leaving clapped him on the shoulder.

"Wonderful, terrific, thanks," they said.

"Don't mention it," he growled. "Come tomorrow night, same time, same place." Crack of glass, jingle of a piece that made it into the bag with the others.

Asa stayed in his chair. He could have taken the broom that rested at the far edge of the garage and swept the butts from the edge of the pool, but he didn't. He could have joined Roberto and saved the remaining pieces of glass from being crushed into sand, but he didn't do that either. There was no point to Roberto's cleaning. In the morning Lolly, their pale servant, would clean everything. Roberto only started to clean when he wanted the party to end.

"Roberto, cut out the cleaning," said Parker, who had walked Amy to the end of the driveway and kissed her until they were both out of breath, and returned with a hot face and a happy self-absorption.

"Why don't *you* clean something up, Whiting," Roberto said. "Sweep up the butts."

"Oh, let Lolly do it," Parker said. He yawned and flopped onto the deck chair next to Asa's. "Sulking?" he asked.

"Yeah, I'm sulking," said Asa.

"Did you find Lydia?"

"I didn't look for her."

"Who's Lydia?" asked Roberto.

"Never mind. Forget it." Asa got out of his chair. It felt strange to be standing up. The blood whizzed up and down his legs in a peculiar way that made him queasy.

"Great party," said Parker, after a minute of silence. "Don't you think?"

"I thought it stunk," said Roberto.

"How about you, Asa?"

"Fine," said Asa.

"Lively bunch here." Parker sank back in the chair and went to sleep.

Roberto had finished with the glass and was walking around the pool picking up cigarette butts. Parker wheezed and opened his mouth, but kept sleeping. Asa stood on his tingling legs in the shadows and hated everything. He hated Parker for being able to sleep and for being able to find a girl who would kiss him more than once. He hated Roberto for making everyone feel guilty by cleaning up. He hated himself for sulking, for wanting what he couldn't have, and for not being dignified enough to have punched Roberto when he called him a ghost. He hated the party for being over and for having ever begun, and the night for its thick, cricket-crazy air, and the pool for its imperturbable surface, which he envied, and Professor Sola for his secret Grace, and Reuben—Reuben who wasn't even there to be hated—he hated simply for being himself, that self which, in its blare and blaze of assurance, could draw all eyes and hands as a fire.

Suddenly the four spotlights on the garage roof came on. The terrace, the pool, and half the lawn were under their white auspices. They were so bright that they gave all objects a vibrating aura—metal in particular changed its character. The legs of chairs and the three-step ladder leading into the shallow end of the pool quivered and shot out white-green penumbras, as though the light were a new element that had altered their composition and transformed them into slices of comets or stars—something, at any rate, that burned hot and fierce. The light made confusion out of living things, isolating each movement, so that Roberto, bending down to gather trash, was kin to a time-lapse photograph of a ballet dancer, a series of postures living in ghostly yet vivid sequence, dozens of Robertos shimmering around the real Roberto hidden in the middle of his duplicates. Even Parker asleep had twenty rising and falling chests.

"For Chrissake, turn the lights off!" yelled Roberto. "You'll scare the neighborhood."

Reuben, wearing nothing at all, burst out of the garage and into the pool. He was a huge white fish underwater for the whole length of it. At the deep end he darted up, pulling his torso out of the water, and yelled, "Fuck the neighborhood!" He went down again, he turned somersaults, he splashed Roberto on purpose. After five minutes of this, satisfied, he catapulted over the ladder and stood on the flagstones, shaking himself like a dog while the water ran down him in green and ash-white streams. "I'm going to be seventeen," he cried, raising his arms to the night sky. "Seventeen."

Asa took his bike from the bushes and rode home.

THE ANGEL OF
MONADNOCK
II

The rest of the summer passed uneventfully; there were no more parties, and Jo took Reuben sailing on the weekends, leaving Parker, Asa, and Roberto to sit by the pool during the dog days. The second tall building remained a hole in the ground and Reuben's plan for the four of them to make a big climb remained just a plan. By September all of them were ready for a change. Their sweaters and scarves looked like Christmas presents—new and unusual—when they came out of the cedar trunks where they'd been laid in April. Dr. Thayer took Asa to Brooks Brothers and bought him a dark blue cashmere coat that came to his knees and had a flap to hide the buttons; it was his first overcoat and, according to his father, his last. Standing at his mirror late at night he tried it on and pretended he was a playboy, with his suntanned skin against the heavy, deeply colored collar. In St. Moritz for the day, back from the Bahamas—he walked back and forth in front of the mirror hoping to catch himself unawares in it and find himself also new and unusual.

On September 15, the group went down to the Back Bay Station together—except Roberto, who was staying in Cambridge to redo his final year at a cram house called Manter Hall. More than Reuben, Roberto was incapable of putting his heart into school; he had been dismissed from Andover in the middle of his senior year for cheating on a Latin test. Like mother and money, this was not a topic for discussion. In fact, the first Asa heard of it was at the beginning of September, when Roberto started classes. Manter Hall was in the middle of Harvard Square and was filled with "problem" boys whose parents were determined that they go to acceptable colleges. The school offered facts and numbers and topic sentences; there was no pretense of inspiring the students, much less making gentlemen of them. Roberto rode Reuben's ten-speed in the mornings and sat on the Eliot House lawn to eat his lunch in isolation. At week's end he was quizzed by his adviser and, after dinner, by his troubled father, who concluded each session by asking how he had produced two dullards and what he was going to do about them.

So Roberto, now in a permanent sulk, was cramming the binomial theorem at ten-fifteen in the morning when Reuben, Parker, and Asa stood in a knot amid hundreds of others heading north and south to school.

Asa wore his coat despite the balmy amber weather. Reuben was wearing a white T-shirt against all regulations ("Andover students are expected to wear jackets and ties at all times when school is in session except in their private rooms"). Parker wore Clem's outgrown Harris tweed sportcoat, which was baggy but sophisticated. They didn't speak much. Reuben fiddled with his racquet press and wondered aloud if the Spaniard with the terrific serve would be returning. "You're such a jock," snapped Asa, who hated tennis and was tired of watching Reuben dash off to games with Jo, practice his backhand off the garage, and buy five pairs of white shorts and white socks in a ten-minute trip to J. August, Clothiers to Gentlemen. He had dragged Asa along. Reuben had taken large bills from his wallet and handed them to the cashier without looking, the way Asa's father paid for dinner when he and Asa's mother came for Parents' Weekend at Choate; it made Asa nervous to watch Reuben flipping twenties in and out of his pocket. The differences between their lives seemed to be growing. And yet, here in the station, where the sun streaked the floor with dust-infused stripes, where the pigeons who roosted in the painted plaster ceiling swooped down after a dropped piece of raisin bun, where all the young men of good family in the Boston area stood stiff in new khakis, Reuben was everything familiar and comfortable, and Asa hated leaving him and their wonderful, pointless, seemingly endless but now ending summer.

Asa and Parker had taken up smoking during the heat spell when Reuben was off on the Bay in Jo's boats, and they now lighted their last Pall Malls of the season with Parker's Zippo, which he'd "clipped" (his new word) from his father's bureau. Reuben was scornful. "You guys are idiots," he said. He had stopped smoking because he didn't want to impair his lung capacity. This reason, repeated whenever they lit up, made the smokers giggle each time they heard it. "Oh, stop it," Reuben said.

"What? Smoking?" Parker blew some rings; he was good at it.

"You know, your father's the one who told me it impairs your lung capacity." Reuben put his hand on Asa's cashmere arm.

"Yes, it sounds just like him," said Asa. He inhaled and felt the dusty rasp of tobacco traveling down his throat. He loved smoking. It made him aware of every breath, of the dimensions of his insides, of the taste of his mouth and lips, of the way his hand held and moved objects. He put a cloud of smoke between himself and Reuben. Reuben could be anybody, a stick figure in a drawing, a fifth former he didn't know. . . . The train to Wallingford was called.

The Choate-bound boys grabbed their suitcases and ran for the stairs, turning at the top to wave to Reuben, who had to wait for the shuttle to North Station. He was standing alone in the space the three of them had carved out, between two sunbeams. He put his tennis racquet up in front of his face so he looked like a dog in a pound, or a prisoner pressing on his bars. "Live it up!" he yelled. "Give 'em hell!" Then he raised the racquet high and served an imaginary ball in their direction. The crowd pressed them down the stairs to the track, where the air smelled of steam and hot metal and winter was on the heels of the breeze that funneled into the tunnel.

Toward the end of October, when the days had been truncated by the turning back of the clocks, Asa returned to his triple after European history to find a letter from Reuben. It was a four-line note that read:

Dear Asa, I'm taking five courses and playing soccer. I'm flunking four of them but still counting on you as my Harvard roommate. Come up and cheer for me next weekend when we play Exeter. I'll meet 11:20 train on Saturday.

R.

How like him to assume I'll come, thought Asa, but already he'd begun to tally up his clean socks and consider what books he'd take to study on the train. He rummaged on top of Parker's desk to see if he had also gotten an invitation, and was happy to find he hadn't. Parker was wearing a bit thin on Asa. He insisted on smoking in their rooms, which was grounds for expulsion, he made piles of clothes at the foot of his bed, which smelled long before he got around to taking them to the laundry, and he was under the spell of Baudelaire, whom he quoted unceasingly in French. Harrison Grey, the other roommate, had exchanged his seersucker suit for gray flannel but was as dull as ever. He was dull-witted as well, and had to study hard; every evening he sat with a straight back at his desk and read while Parker tried to distract him.

"Paris change! mais rien dans ma mélancolie n'a bougé," Parker would intone, flinging open the windows that gave onto the peaceful Connecticut fields. Then, standing behind

Harrison's flannel back, "Hypocrite lecteur,—mon sembla-ble,—mon frère." None of this had any effect on Harrison, who took German not French, but it drove Asa to the library for peace.

In the library Asa daydreamed. He preferred to read lying down, and to write his papers late at night, so there was little for him to do in the library. He thought about Reuben. At first it seemed he was thinking about the summer; he remembered the glittering water and the feel of the canvas chair against the backs of his knees, and contrasted it with the beige spiky trees clustered outside the long library windows and the mahogany chair where he sat and watched those trees lose their leaves. But in his thoughts Reuben was always sitting in a deck chair beside him, and they were planning escapades, or parties, exchanging stories about girls (something they never did in reality), getting to know each other. For Asa had realized that they didn't know each other. Friendship in his little gang consisted of Parker and Asa vying for Reuben's attention and thinking of subtle ways to exclude Roberto. Asa wondered: Did Reuben know he was the focus and that this kept the others divided? Asa decided that Reuben might not only know this but have manufactured it himself. On the other hand, it was possible that he was oblivious, as he pretended to be. But didn't that oblivion contain a sort of natural arrogance and pride, which took for granted rivalries and jealousy? Perhaps that was why Reuben had gravitated to Jo; he could have conversations with her. But Reuben lying blond and warm on the deck of a boat with Jo had not been seeking a conversation. Asa remembered Jo's hand on Reuben's bony wrist in the car, and the mixed-up taste of Jo's mouth—the conversations those two had were silent, also of a sort Reuben couldn't have with Asa.

Asa tipped his chair back and watched rain moving in over

the tops of trees. He wanted someone to talk to about how he felt watching trees in the rain, which was sad and delighted and hollow, as if his insides had become a receptacle for emotions that floated in the air, looking for a resting place. Parker looking at trees felt he was Baudelaire; what Asa wondered was how Reuben felt. Did he ever stop to look at trees?

So the invitation was opportune, because Asa needed to know more about Reuben. He packed his changes of socks and Ovid's *Metamorphoses,* put *The Mayor of Casterbridge* in the pocket of his cashmere coat, and set out early on Saturday morning by train, which sped along the flat, frost-encrusted lower New England seashore stirring flocks of small gray gulls with its approach. At the Back Bay Station he was a tourist waiting for the shuttle to North Station and another train to take him further up. This train passed through still mill towns where long, black factories with broken windows hunched empty. Asa had enough history to know that only fifty years before, cousins of his had overseen cousins of Reuben's as they bent over looms in these mills. Or was he mistaken, and did Jews not have cousins? His impression of Jews was that like his own class they were a small group given to marrying each other and avoiding outsiders; such behavior led to a multitude of cousins. He decided to ask Reuben about the family arrangements of Jews.

At Andover everything looked exactly as it looked in Wallingford. There were white houses ringed around a common thick with beeches and oaks; there were fewer than seven shops, and those sold either food, books, or pharmaceuticals; there were handsome dogs sporting on the brown lawns. Waiting for the train to stop moving so he could descend, Asa had a moment of envying Roberto, who had all of Harvard Square to prowl through on his way to and from school.

Why was it a privilege to be hidden away in these sleepy country towns?

Reuben was leaning against the side of the ticket booth. For once he was dressed correctly, in a blue-gray tweed jacket, blue tie with white stripes, white shirt, and charcoal-gray pants. His clothes were of excellent quality and excellently tailored, but he seemed to be wearing a costume. Asa stopped at the top step and looked Reuben over, wondering how he managed to appear oddly dressed in what was, after all, the term-time uniform of everyone the two of them knew. It was the sneakers, Asa decided. Reuben wore once-white sneakers so old that his little toes popped through on both feet. Asa wore cordovans his father had bought him in tenth grade, which he hated because the color reminded him of slaughtering chickens with his grandfather. His father had said, as when he'd bought the cashmere coat, "These will last for the rest of your life." It appeared he was right. Asa's cordovans trod the grimy steel steps of the train down to the platform and went to Reuben's side.

The game began at one, so they went immediately to the dining hall, where a number of people said hello to Reuben. Asa hoped to be introduced but wasn't. Then Reuben put Asa in an armchair in the library, gave him instructions to the playing fields (the grounds were enormous, far larger than Choate's), and hurried to his pregame strategy meeting in the locker room. "Sit on the right side," he called from the door, "that's our side." Asa read *The Mayor of Casterbridge* for a while and fell asleep. He had been up at six, and was accustomed to rising at seven-thirty; that tiredness combined with the lulling movement of the train, which persisted in his body, the chicken pie filled mostly with potatoes, and the deliberate unrolling of Hardy's plot to stupefy him. He slept for a long time. When he woke up the sun was lower, brighter, and shining in a different window. He pulled out his pocket watch: three o'clock. Over the tops of trees, muted by the carpets in the library but clear and high, yells came from the direction Reuben had pointed him in hours before. Asa jumped out of his chair and began formulating excuses. I'll just tell him I couldn't get through the crowds to him, he thought. The first order of business, though, was to find out who'd won the game. Then he could make his way to the locker room with congratulations or comfort.

He put on his coat and went outside under the elms flanking the library to overhear the news. It was clear that Andover had trounced Exeter. The yellow buses at the foot of the great lawn, which had brought the Exeter team and boosters, were filling with quiet pairs of boys; shirt-sleeved Andoverites were doing handsprings and somersaults on the stubbly grass. Asa went up to some boys standing near him who were describing the game play-by-play to each other, relishing their favorite moments.

"Can you tell me how to get to the locker room?" he asked.

"You from Exeter?" Everybody looked at him intently.

"No, Choate. I'm a friend of somebody on your team."

"Who?" The one asking didn't relax his suspiciousness, although the others seemed prepared to go back to their game review. He peered through his gold rims as though he suspected Asa of being a spy.

"Sola," said Asa.

"What position does he play?" Gold Rims, Asa could see, had decided to make sport by grilling him. This was precisely the question he hadn't wanted to be asked, because he hadn't a clue to what position Reuben played.

"Oh, leave him alone, Bowditch. I know Sola, he's left wing," one of the calmer boys said. "The gym is about three minutes that way, and the locker room's on your right." He pointed past the library. "Tell him he made a terrific goal there, at the end."

"Thanks," said Asa. He buttoned his coat up and set off, pleased to have gotten two unexpected and useful pieces of information. He could congratulate Reuben on his goal.

But when he got to the locker room and saw Reuben stripped and shiny among all the others, he didn't want to lie. Reuben asked how he'd enjoyed himself, and Asa said, "I fell asleep and missed the whole thing."

"Wonderful," Reuben said. "Just the thing to do. Not worth watching anyhow. It's fun to play, but I don't bother going to games I'm not in. It's cold and boring." He combed his wet hair back from his forehead with a small tortoiseshell comb that had a gold edge and looked as if it belonged to a woman. "Hold on a second, I'll be dressed and we can go have something hot." He winked; Asa wondered if he had a booze cache somewhere and supposed so.

"That's a very nice comb," Asa said. Some demon motivated him; he knew it would be the wrong thing to say. Sure enough, Reuben's face became blank and stiff.

"Thanks," he said, and slipped it quickly into the pocket of his pants, which were still hanging in his locker.

"Was it your mother's?" Asa persisted. He amazed himself; he couldn't imagine why he was pursuing this dangerous topic, but his resolve to "get closer" to Reuben and to find out about Jewish family affairs seemed to justify snooping.

"Forget it," said Reuben. "Go outside and wait for me." Asa obeyed. Reuben kept him waiting fifteen minutes as punishment. Asa used the time to formulate more invasive questions, which he resolved to ask late at night, when Reuben was tired. Who was your mother? he would ask, and, Why is she never discussed? What is your father really like? and,

Who is Grace? How much money do you have? Where are your cousins? Do you have grandparents? How many kisses, and what besides kisses, have you and Jo exchanged? Do you prefer Parker to me? When he reached this question Asa realized he probably wouldn't ask any of the questions. He resolved not to be petulant. After all, he, not Parker, was waiting for Reuben. He wondered why the answers to these questions interested him as much as they did.

He thought perhaps the way to find the answers was to confide in Reuben; after all, their ignorance extended both ways. Reuben didn't know about the whore in June, or Mrs. Thayer's two stillborn children, one before, one after, Asa. These two pieces of information didn't seem as thrilling as the information Asa was looking for, but that might be because he possessed them already. Maybe Reuben would find them valuable. He could only offer them and see what happened.

It was dark and chilly outside on the northern wall of the gym, facing the fields and woods whose feathery outlines Asa could no longer see. He had a sense of having traveled north, and this made him long for New Hampshire. Thanksgiving would be at his grandparents' farm as usual, and he had a vivid memory of tramping through icy mud in the morning to fetch eggs for breakfast from under the warm hens. He liked the cleanness of winter, the way the air was purified and thinned until it became nearly painful to breathe. He took a deep breath, waiting for the minty sharpness of the air, but October was too early for that. And then Reuben came out, with a mist of heat around him and his jacket open, and took Asa's arm, so that Asa's solitude was melted. They walked arm in arm back to the dining hall through the moist leaves that clung to the paths.

This time Reuben introduced Asa to a few of the people who greeted him in the food line. But he steered them to a table in the corner that was unoccupied except for a thin, pale-brown boy bent over a plate of steak and potato. This fellow, who rose as they approached, was too tall for himself—his cuffs had not kept pace with his arms, and he wobbled when he stood, so Asa imagined he'd shot up five inches overnight and hadn't adjusted. All his features were watered-down hazel and looked unhealthy; his hair was slicked sideways with an unguent that gave off an unpleasant glow, his eyes were bloodshot, and his face was nicked and chipped from acne. Instead of a tie he wore a red polka-dotted ascot. To Asa's surprise, Reuben clapped this character on the shoulder and introduced him enthusiastically.

"Kuhn," he said, "meet Asa Thayer, my companion in Cambridge. This is Jerry Kuhn, without whom Andover would be unbearable."

Asa looked at Jerry Kuhn and wondered how he could improve Andover so much, then looked around the dining hall, wondering what had to be improved. It was a larger, more pleasant dining hall than Choate's, because it was older and therefore had wood paneling, two chandeliers, and decent refectory tables. Choate had in the past five years been given an anonymous million and spent it on building a few new, ugly buildings, one of which was a dining hall with pastel walls and Formica-topped tables for easy cleaning. Asa much preferred this, which was an inflated version of his dining room at home. For that matter, it wasn't very different from Reuben's dining room. As to Kuhn, Asa couldn't imagine what he had to offer. He felt himself sinking into a sulk, but was unable to stop it.

The two of them were full of chat. Reuben was ribbed

about being a "jock," about his having saved the team's honor with his goal, and then about his clothes.

"You are really looking the part tonight—expecting somebody to take your picture for the yearbook? I see you've got your Andover tie on, that's the school spirit we like to see here. Nice cloth"—Kuhn's long finger massaged Reuben's collar—"have that made up for you at Brooks by the dozen, eh?"

"Jerry, you're the worst snob on campus," said Reuben cheerfully. He put a potato skin in his mouth and pulled it across his front teeth to extract all the pulp. Asa was glad to see his table manners weren't any better at school than at home. But apparently Jerry found them offensive.

"Christ almighty, learn to eat with your mouth shut, man, or you'll never be part of the ruling class."

"Is that what I'm aiming for?" Reuben asked. They both laughed. Asa, not wanting to be left out, laughed as well, but he felt on dangerous ground. What was he laughing at? One must eat with a shut mouth. That was common knowledge. On the other hand, he took a mystifying but real pleasure in Reuben's flouting of these fundamental rules; perhaps Jerry shared this pleasure, and it made him laugh. Reuben was satisfying because he didn't bother with table manners, proper shoes, or proper grades—but Asa assumed this was by choice, not because he was incapable or ignorant. Reuben's knowing better and behaving worse took courage.

Reuben said, with his mouth full, "I am in the ruling class, Jerry, and don't you forget it." Jerry laughed some more and Asa stared at his plate where a half moon of fat was turning hard.

"Money's only half of it. Around here it won't even get you in the door. Or just in the door. None of these fellows has any money." Jerry waved his arm at the ranks of tweed backs. "They pride themselves on not having any money." He turned to Asa. "How much money do you have at your disposal?"

Asa bristled. This was one of the questions he was meaning to ask Reuben, but it was entirely different to have it posed by a stranger. "Not much," he said evenly, and hoped he'd covered the topic. But he hadn't.

"And how much is that?"

"Well, nothing, unless I ask for it."

"Aha," said Jerry.

"Come on," Reuben said, "you've got an allowance or something, don't you?"

"No, I've got what I earned last summer, and my mother sends me fifteen dollars a month out of that." They stared. "It's not like I need money for anything," Asa said. "What would I get?"

"Cigarettes," said Reuben.

"Books," said Jerry.

"Booze," said Reuben.

"Tickets to the movies," said Jerry.

"I can't smoke at school," said Asa sadly. He missed it. "How about you?" He looked at Reuben beside him, with gravy on his shirt. "What have you got?"

"Oh, Jesus, I don't know. I have a checking account, and my father, or the bank, or someone, drops two hundred dollars a month into it."

"Two hundred dollars a month!" Asa leaned back in his chair. "You could—you could go around the world!"

"If I saved it," Reuben agreed. "But I don't save it. I get stuff."

"Like the car?"

"Oh no, Father got me that. Like these." He shot his cuffs and showed Asa gold and mother-of-pearl cuff links in the shape of grape leaves.

"And they're absolutely hideous," Jerry said. "You have no business wasting your money on horrible things. You ought at least to have some taste. Why don't you take this young fellow with you when you get the urge to spend? He looks like a fellow of taste. Look at that nice coat. He wouldn't let you buy these atrocities."

Asa bristled again at being called a young fellow by another young fellow, but was glad Jerry appreciated the coat. Still, he didn't like the conversation. He didn't like Jerry, either. "How much money do *you* have?" he asked sharply.

"I'm somewhere between the two of you. I don't have a fortune like Mr. Sola. On the other hand I don't have cold, grasping Yankee parents who won't give me enough to take my pals to the show. I assume your family is well-heeled enough to have bought that coat new? It isn't something you found at Keezer's?"

"What's Keezer's?"

"Point made," said Jerry.

"And how do you know my parents are cold and grasping?" Asa said this in such a halfhearted way that Reuben put an arm around him.

"Don't take offense at Jerry," he said. "Jerry isn't well brought up. He doesn't know anything about your parents, he's just making unpleasant generalizations."

"But Reuben, they dole out his own money to him, money he earned, for heaven's sake, and they made him go out and earn it in the first place—"

"They didn't. I wanted to. I was sick of being sent off to the country, so I stayed in town and worked."

"No matter. It's your money, and you shouldn't have to

wait for them to give it to you. Don't you think I'm right?"

Asa thought about it. He looked at his blood-red shoes and pondered. Jerry said softly to Reuben, "Portrait of a Yankee thinking." Asa looked up, hurt.

"Yes, I think you're right, but I don't think my parents would go along with it. And it's not worth fighting about."

"What is worth fighting about? What do you fight with your parents about?"

"I try not to. I mean, it wears me out. I'm not there most of the time . . ." This reminded him of a conversation he'd had with Parker during the summer. "I hate fighting," he said.

"I rather enjoy it," Jerry said, and he leaned back in his chair, triumphant. "And you're not bad at it either, Sola."

"Oh, I usually leave it to Roberto. Roberto and Papa have a battle going over honesty, so when I turn up I look like the good boy, which is fine. I'm sick of fighting. I've done plenty."

"But you're always doing things that will get you into trouble," Asa said.

"It doesn't matter. I'm the good son. I can do anything."

"I wish that would happen to me," Asa said. "That's the trouble with being an only child, you're always the bad one."

"Or the good one," Jerry said. "I'm the only son, and so I'm always the good son. My sisters can never be boys, so they've failed from the start. Every mother needs a little messiah of her own."

"That's an interesting point," Reuben said. Asa thought it was a crazy point; actually, he didn't even think it was a point. But Reuben was chewing over this "point" with fascination. "I think you're right, I think that's the way it is."

"But you don't even have a mother," Asa protested.

"Everybody has a mother to start with," Jerry said, "even Reuben."

"And she thought you were—" Asa couldn't get the words out.

"Oh no, she wasn't of that persuasion." Reuben smiled at Jerry. "But I've seen it in other families."

Asa made a lunge in the direction he thought Reuben had pointed in. "You mean she wasn't Jewish?"

Jerry folded his napkin into a tiny square; Reuben ate his cold, withered potato skin. But Asa, who had decided he too had a right to ask insulting questions, refused to be daunted. He felt himself momentarily in ascendance over them and repeated his question. "Was she?"

Reuben turned his blank, ice-blond face toward Asa and said, "Yes, she was." Then he got up and went to a table where apple pie was being topped off with vanilla ice cream by a starchy kitchen aide. Asa waited for a confidence from Jerry; surely he would lean across the table and explain, in two hurried sentences, why Reuben didn't talk about his mother. Jerry sat straight, worrying his napkin as if he were folding the secret into the linen so it couldn't get out, and didn't say anything. Reuben came back with pie, which they ate without talking.

"Let's have coffee. Let's go into town," Reuben said when he'd finished his pie.

"Can we do that?" Asa asked. Wallingford was off limits to Choate students; it required the same signed permission slip to walk into town as to take the train to Boston.

"Who's going to stop us?" asked Jerry. "They've got better things to do than keep track of seniors. Put on your coat." He leaned across the table, as he had to touch Reuben's collar, and stroked the sleeve. "Let me try it on."

"It won't fit you," said Asa promptly. He smiled at Jerry, but Jerry had stood up and was staring at the coat. "It won't fit at all."

"I'm not buying it, for Chrissake, I just want to try it on."

Reuben yawned and raised his arms above his head. "I'm going to get a black leather jacket during vacation. With a big silver zipper. I think it'll look good with my car."

Asa was defeated; the jacket would supersede the cashmere coat, and he would find himself one step behind, as usual. He passed the coat over the sticky plates to Jerry. The coat transformed Jerry's awkwardness into length and grace, and imparted an air of importance to his pallid, pocked face. "Gee, you look terrific in that coat," Asa said, despite himself.

"Not my style," Jerry said, but he didn't take it off. He buttoned it and pushed his hands into the pockets. "Well, it's warm. But doesn't it make you look like a banker? I'm getting a trench coat—pockets and flaps and buckles."

"You'll look like a spy. Is that better than a banker?" Reuben asked.

Asa wanted his coat back. He moved from one foot to another and stared into space and wondered why he felt irritated and left out. Irritated—because he wanted his coat; that was simple. Also because his coat was being maligned, though he could tell Jerry liked it. It was Jerry who looked like a banker, Asa decided. Asa in his coat looked like a young man in prep school; his posturing in front of the mirror had been unconvincing. He was no playboy. Reuben, however, might transform the coat into an emblem of elegance; Reuben seemed to be more powerful than what he wore. Asa decided to offer Reuben the coat. That would get it away from Jerry and bring him closer to Reuben, which would, possibly, ease the feeling of being left out.

"Why don't you try it?" he said. "I bet you won't look like a banker in it."

"Oh, let's just go get some fucking coffee," said Reuben. "Let's just go. I can't stand this place another minute." His face was pale and pinched, and he looked like his father for a minute, tightening his lips and grinding his teeth. Asa heard the faint crackle of his jaws moving. It was a distinctive Sola sound. They all did it when irked. Roberto had spent three years in braces to correct the injuries he'd inflicted on his bite; Reuben had knots of muscle at the base of his cheeks that bulged and trembled; Professor Sola sometimes sounded like a firecracker as he shuffled down the hall gnashing on the cud of his private rages.

What was bothering them? wondered Asa. Why were they such a nervous family? His family did not grind teeth, flunk courses, sulk, glower, whisper things to water. In his family everything went according to schedule and everything was as it should be. If Asa were to go to Princeton rather than Harvard, dinner might be more silent than usual for a few evenings, but there would not be scenes, there would not be people snarling in hallways, banging doors, or any of the other peculiar things he had seen at the Solas'. Asa had eaten a meal there in which Professor Sola addressed all his remarks to Roberto via Reuben, in the third person: "Does he think he's going to get into college by virtue of his blond hair?" "Does he want more salad?" Reuben, playing according to the rules of this bizarre game, would repeat the question to Roberto, receive an answer, and repeat the answer, again in the third person, to their father. Asa was fascinated and uneasy. Neither of the boys had commented on it, and two days later everything was back to normal.

Reuben crunched vehemently. Jerry gave the coat back to Asa. They pushed their chairs up to the table, strode out of the dining hall ("The thing is to look innocent and determined," Reuben whispered), and cut straight across the broad, brown lawn to the road into town. They turned right and walked downhill, Reuben and Jerry side by side, Asa bobbing behind them, sometimes inserting his shoulder between them, more often kept back by the narrowness of the sidewalk.

After ten minutes of this they reached town, not a minute too soon for Asa, who wanted to flag down a passing bus or slouch off to the train station in the dark. Reuben could send him his socks and his toothbrush—he was not going to trail along like a baby brother. But there was the coffee shop, and Reuben holding the door open for him; maybe on the way back it would be Jerry who walked behind.

The coffee shop was in the back of a drugstore with high shelves ranked with blue glass bottles that read DIGITALIS and PEROXIDE in gold letters. "They put arsenic in the coffee," Reuben said. Asa believed it. They were served their coffee in thick, white porcelain mugs with the Andover seal. Reuben took a flask from his pocket and put a large shot into his coffee without offering it around. Neither the proprietor, a fat person who looked as though he'd been dipped in talcum powder, nor Jerry took any notice.

Asa draped his coat over a stool and *The Mayor of Caster-bridge* fell out of the pocket. Jerry jumped off his stool and snatched it up before Asa had a chance to move.

"You like this? It's his worst. You ought to be reading *Tess.*"

"It's assigned."

"Why do they always assign the worst ones? I bet you've read *Adam Bede* and hated it. Right?"

"Yes. Last year."

"Read *Tess,* read *Jude,* read *Daniel Deronda*—yes, read that. That will tell you something about the Jews."

"I have too much reading to do already," Asa said. "I have to read the *Metamorphoses* by Wednesday."

"In Latin?"

"No."

"It's better in Latin." Jerry had opened the book and was leafing through it as if it were a picture album. "It's plodding, it's safe, there's more to Hardy than this."

"No literature," Reuben mumbled. He was bent over his coffee to inhale the evaporating brandy. "Fuck Hardy. Fuck the Jews in England and Victorian morality." He put another shot in his cup. "I can't wait to get to college. I'm so sick of this place—it's dead. Thayer—" Asa winced. When Reuben called him Thayer it was a sign that a black, remote mood was coming on, one that Reuben would intensify by picking fights and increasing his isolation. "Thayer, if we were in Cambridge, we could go looking for bicycles to steal, you know? We could go down to the Casablanca and see how many drinks we could handle, and whether we could get somebody else to pay for them. We could drive out to the airport and watch the planes take off. No end of entertainment in dear old Cambridge."

"Sounds like the pastimes of a gang of hoodlums," Jerry said.

"What do you know? You live in some suburb that tries to look just like this place, where you sit around talking books with your parents after dinner. Did you know that Jerry's parents are Communists?" He leaned toward Asa.

"No."

"No, you didn't know? No, they can't be? Explain yourself."

"No, I didn't know," said Asa. Reuben's face was very close to his own and gave off a slight smell of liquor. His eyes were elongated and somewhat Orientalized from drinking and tiredness, his mouth had become thin and venomous—altogether he looked, Asa decided, like a thin and angry version of the man-in-the-moon: inscrutable, dangerous, and pseudohuman. "How remarkable," Asa said, hoping this would draw Jerry out and shift the focus away from Reuben.

"How remarkable—who are you? Are you your mother? God, what a half-ass town this is," snarled Reuben. "The place is infectious. Everybody here says things like that, 'How remarkable.' If the bomb went off, the whole senior class would get to its feet and say in unison, 'How really remarkable,' and then drop dead."

"I'd rather talk about literature than listen to you knocking Andover," Jerry said.

"Of course you would, but that's too bad. I've listened to you talk about literature for two years."

"You had plenty to say yourself."

"I've said it. I'm not saying another word about literature." Reuben tipped his flask to his cup again, but nothing came out. "Shit," he said softly. "Oh, well, time to get back."

Asa obediently rose to his feet.

"Really, why does it always have to be your timetable?" Jerry said. "I'm still drinking my coffee."

"Nobody's stopping you," said Reuben. He didn't get up either. Asa shifted his feet around and put his coat on, then got back on his stool.

"Thayer," Jerry said, to nobody in particular. "Thayer, now why does that sound familiar?"

"Just one of those names," Reuben said. "Just one of those crazy names." He hummed to the appropriate tune. "Those Yankee names, you know?"

"No, it's something more specific."

"I probably have some cousins here," said Asa. "Actually, I do have one, he's in one of the lower forms, his name is Dana, I think he's eleven—"

"I've got it! It's that painting." Jerry turned to look at Asa.

"It's not a bad painting, by Thayer. Abbott Thayer. And you know, it looks a bit like you. Doesn't it?" He poked Reuben's shoulder. "Look at him."

"I've seen him," said Reuben.

"Look, he looks like it."

"Probably a cousin," said Reuben, with a grin.

"Don't you have any cousins?" asked Asa, surprised at what a lucky opportunity he'd been given. Reuben didn't bother to answer him.

"Jews don't have cousins," said Jerry. "All Jewish cousins are dead. But I think we ought to go see this painting."

"Where is it?" Asa asked. He hoped it was somewhere far away so the whole thing would be forgotten in the morning.

"It's right next to the library, in the museum."

"Oh, well, then it's shut," said Asa.

"We'll break in," Reuben said, sitting up and opening his eyes. "We'll be in there before you know it. There's a skylight that can't be locked above the stairwell. We can just drop down—all we need is rope." He rapped his spoon on the thick handle of his coffee cup to rouse the powdery proprietor. "Got any rope for sale?" The proprietor drew a ball of string from under the counter. "No, rope, like for rock climbing."

"You'd have to get that at McBurr's," he said.

"We could break in there," Reuben said. "It's just down the block."

"They'll be open at eight," said the proprietor. "Gotta climb that rock tonight?"

"I'll find some at the gym." Reuben put his flask in his pocket and stood up. "Let's go. I'm sure there's rope at the gym."

This time, as Asa had hoped, it was Jerry who trailed behind; Reuben actually put his arm through Asa's. Asa could feel Reuben's muscles quivering. He talked the whole way up the hill about his plan for getting them in. "I'll do the entering, then I'll open the door for you guys. You softies won't want to drop down on a rope, I guess. But you might have to—the door might be wired or something. We'll see. It'll be easy. I've thought of doing it many times."

"Why?" asked Asa.

"Steal some art. Raise a ruckus. Mainly because it occurred to me that it could be done." He detached himself from Asa and stepped into the road. "Never pass up a challenge," he yelled. Then he returned to the sidewalk. "That's why."

At the gym there was enough rope to hang them all, thought Asa grimly. Now that the expedition was inevitable, he tried to show some interest in it. "What's the name of the painting?"

"The Monadnock Angel," Jerry said.

Asa got a chill down his back. He didn't want to be like an angel; it was reminiscent of being a ghost. And Monadnock was the mountain that shadowed his grandparents' farm. "This guy's name is Thayer? You're sure?"

"He's almost famous. Abbott Thayer. He lived up there. They have a number of his paintings here, I don't know why."

"He probably went here," said Asa.

"Artists don't go to Andover," said Reuben, winding up rope.

The stars had gone out and the whole school had gone to sleep when the three emerged from the gym. It was cold, much colder than it had been during the day, and the leaves left on the trees crackled when the wind shook them. Asa turned up the collar of his coat. "Don't talk," whispered Reuben. "I'll lead. When we get there, I'll tell you what to do." They walked single file down the path. At the museum

Reuben drew them into the shadow of a large, dead bush.

"You'll give me a leg up, hoist me up to that window," he pointed to the sill of an arched, leaded window about five feet above the ground, "and then throw me the rope. Up above there's a ledge with a little roof. That's where the skylight is. You'll be able to see me through the window, so you'll know when to go to the door. If I don't open the door in five minutes after I've gotten inside, you'll know it's wired. Then come back here and I'll pull you up by the rope."

"It just doesn't look possible," Asa said. "Let's come back tomorrow. It's open on Sunday, isn't it?"

"Yes," Jerry said. "How about it, Reuben? I don't think we can lift you all the way up to that window."

"Come *on,*" said Reuben. "Come on, guys, you don't have to do anything except give me a leg up. Jesus, can't you just do that? I'm sure the door isn't wired. You'll be able to walk right in."

So they made a brace of their hands and arms, and Reuben hopped onto it. He was surprisingly light, Asa thought, and as he kept moving, straining his body up and urging them to raise him, he seemed to be flying away from them and to weigh less and less the higher they lifted him. In a matter of seconds he had gained the roof and was poised on the edge of it, prying open the hatchway before they'd had time to disentangle their arms. There was the sound of glass breaking. Reuben's head peeped over the edge: "Had to," he said. "I couldn't undo it." Then there was a creaking, grinding noise as the skylight opened. "Throw me the rope," he said. They couldn't see him.

"Where are you?" hissed Asa.

"Don't worry. Throw it, I'll catch it."

Asa threw and heard it hit the slates; one piece came dislodged and landed in the bush. "Did I make it?" he called.

Reuben's head rose over the edge of the roof again. "Shh. I've got it. Just watch through the window and you'll see me hit the floor. Then go to the door."

Jerry was pacing back and forth. "Do you do things like this all the time in Cambridge? You two seem adept at this kind of stuff."

"Reuben wants to, but I don't. There's another boy, Parker—he likes this sort of thing. They go climbing together, I think. They've stolen things." Asa didn't know any of this to be true, but it felt true, so he said it. Parker and Reuben shared a daredevil streak that left him out, and if the stories he was reporting to Jerry hadn't happened yet, they would happen someday. "We'd better pay attention," he said.

The two of them pressed up to the bottom pane of the window. After a minute the end of the rope came snaking down. About three feet from the floor it stopped. Then it began to ascend. "What's he doing?" asked Jerry. "Probably tying the rope up top," Asa answered. They couldn't see the rope at all for a while, then it was flung down again. This time it reached only to the middle of the window, about seven feet above the floor. A pebble crashed onto the parquet. Then there was silence. Suddenly the rope jerked and started to twirl counterclockwise. "He's on it," said Asa, and held his breath. The rope's shadow drew a dancing, ever-incomplete circle on the floor; Asa thought his lungs would pop, and he couldn't hear Jerry breathing either. And then Reuben's torn sneaker appeared, and its mate, and the cuffs of his gray pants, and the two at the window exhaled, misting the glass with their long-held breath.

Very slowly, as a dream set underwater is slow and thick, the rope lost its tension and the body on it, still twelve or more feet above the floor, began to fall. First the legs lost their grip on the now-slack rope. Then the torso, passing their wide-open eyes as it descended, swung out into space. Then the arms stretched away from the body, flailing and waving. Then the head, fallen onto the chest, eyes shut, mouth open, limp, white, frightful in its blankness, spun past them. Wriggling and whirling, the rope, loosened from above, followed Reuben down like a comet's hairy tail.

"Oh no," screamed Asa, not knowing he was screaming. "Please."

Reuben hit the floor on his hands and knees, the rope fell on his neck, and as he straightened up it draped itself around him so he looked like an animal about to be led somewhere. For a few seconds he stood dumbly, staring off into space. Then he looked out the window, saw their four glazed eyes looking at him, made a V sign with his right hand, and trotted off to open the door.

Asa started laughing and could not stop. Jerry punched him in the arm to startle him out of it, but he continued. "Shut up," said Jerry. "Someone will hear you." Asa laughed and laughed, he doubled over and laughed into the cold earth, he banged on the ground with his hands. "Come on, let's get over to the door," said Jerry, grabbing him and pulling him up.

The effort of walking and laughing simultaneously calmed Asa a little; by the time they'd walked halfway around the building he was just panting softly, simmering with subsiding laughter but paying more attention to getting his breath back. "It wasn't real," he said between gasps, "he was kidding us, wasn't he? He was just scaring us." He grasped his chest with both hands because it hurt. "Oh, God," he said, "I'm so tired."

When they reached the door, it was open, and Reuben was standing on the threshold looking for them. "Asshole," said Jerry. "What the hell was that for?"

"What?" Reuben made his hands into fists and scowled. "What?"

"Forget it," said Asa. "Leave him alone. Let's go see this angel thing." He was still heaving and pressing on his chest with one hand. It was his heart that was hurting him; it seemed to have been pumped up with air and to be taking up more room than was allotted for it in his body.

"It's upstairs," said Jerry.

They tramped upstairs, all of them leaving dirt on the floor. The museum appeared originally to have been a mansion; it had homey touches, fireplaces and wainscoting, that seemed superfluous to a museum. And it smelled like any house on Brattle Street, thought Asa—mixed furniture wax, flowers, discreet amounts of dust. They mounted the stairs, walking through the site of Reuben's fall, or prank, gingerly to avoid the slivers of glass on the floor. "Where is it?" asked Asa.

"Here," said Jerry. They had reached the top of the staircase. On the wall ahead of them was an enormous, dark painting. "I'll get some light." He walked assuredly to the right, found a switch, and flipped it.

The figure was larger than life-size, although Asa wondered if anyone knew an angel's size. Draped in Hellenic robes it rose from a forbidding landscape as familiar to Asa as his backyard, the lumpy, naked ridge of Mount Monadnock. Its wings were half obscured by clouds, its halo dimmed by the bad weather moving in behind it and darkening the earth. Each hand was held at a slight angle away from the body, palms turned outward in the position of forgiveness and acceptance used in Byzantine icons—thumb extended, third and fourth fingers folded in. It was a figure at once static and mobile, being rooted in the rocky land and rising, illuminated, to an illuminated upper atmosphere. Its face was small-mouthed and straight-browed, with an expression at odds with the merciful arrangement of its hands; it looked arrogant and disdainful. And it looked, Asa thought, exactly like Reuben. This seemed so improbable that he looked closer, tracing the shape of its nose and cheeks carefully. This second survey yielded him some understanding of Jerry's contention that it looked like him. The triangular face, the long nose, the broad eyebrows and sharply defined jaw—these were Asa's own. But it had Reuben's flavor. It had passion and it had pride, it had what Asa knew he lacked, what Reuben's father yearned for: Grace.

"I guess it doesn't really look like you that much," said Jerry, startling Asa out of his intent observation. "But a bit, around the jaw. It's certainly got the same coloring you do."

"Well, Reuben has that coloring too," ventured Asa. He wasn't quite prepared to say that he thought this was, in some way, a portrait of Reuben's character.

"Yeah," said Reuben. "I think it looks just as much like me as it does like Asa. Which is to say, Kuhn, that I don't think it has anything to do with either of us. And I think it's a crummy painting. You can't even tell whether the thing is standing on the ground or floating or what." He turned his back on it. "But," he went on, addressing the stairwell, "we got a good adventure out of it."

"Don't you think," said Asa, "don't you think it does look like both of us? I mean as if we'd been mixed together. Like if we'd had a child?"

"What the hell are you talking about?" Reuben said. "Getting bonkers from too many years of prep school? Turning into a pansy?"

"No, no, Reuben, I see what he means," Jerry said. "It's sort of a combination plate of your characteristics; it's got Asa's features and it's got your bad temper—you can see that in its scowl." He laughed.

Reuben turned back to the painting, which he looked at briefly, then looked at Asa, then at Jerry. "I see why you like it," he said to Jerry. "It's a Jewish angel—an avenging angel. It doesn't have that wishy-washy expression you see on Christmas-tree angels. But I think it's a trashy painting; romantic, pseudo-Blake stuff. And yes, it looks like Asa. I'm sure he's a cousin. Now let's go."

"Son of the art collector has spoken," said Jerry. He turned off the light. "I think he used his daughters as models—there are some more conventional portraits in the other room."

Neither Reuben nor Asa had an inclination to go into the other room, Reuben because he wanted to leave, Asa because he did not want to leave off looking at his celestial double. In the now-dim hallway the painting was nearly imperceivable, merely a darker darkness framed in gold, spattered with the occasional glimmers that were the backlit halo and right arm. Reuben was on the landing kicking pieces of gravel around; Jerry had gone into the room where the more conventional portraits were hung. Asa stood undisturbed before the Angel of Monadnock.

But the painting disturbed him. First because he was unable to make a judgment of it as art, whereas Jerry and Reuben could and differed. He told himself it was an excellent painting; that was credible. Then he told himself it was romantic daubing, and that was credible too. Maintaining such a distance from it was difficult, though—he kept being entranced by what it meant rather than by its style. Wasn't that a proof of its claim to being "art"? Maybe only a proof of his sentimentality—that quality responsible for the blocking of his throat and the blurring of his eyes while he looked at the painting, or the dash of his pulse when the train pulled into Andover Station. Likewise for somber yet not unhappy dreams in which he and Jo walked down dark lanes between trees, and Reuben was a badger or an owl or even a stone fence, present but not himself. Asa knew his sentimentality was a poor substitute for passion, although the only way he could formulate this was to deride his life for its safeness and predictability and envy others who surprised themselves, and him, with the way things turned out. "Others" meant Reuben; Parker made attempts to surprise himself, but Asa could too easily project him five years into the future at a desk in his father's law firm. Reuben was unprojectable.

For this reason the painting disturbed him—because while Asa looked at it he had the illusion of seeing himself as a knotty, unpredictable person, although he knew himself to be otherwise. Yet there was his head and his neck (even the outstretched naked arms had dimpled elbows and broad wrists like his), imbued with danger, revenge, authority, and mystery. This was a portrait of his unrealizable ambitions.

Was he to let them go? Ought Reuben to be discarded because he was nothing but a form of self-torture, a way for Asa to have his face rubbed in failure? Alternatively, had he been hoping that Reuben would "rub off" on him? Soberly, he considered the likelihood of his changing into a more compelling, compelled person; he had to admit it was chancy. At Harvard things would be different: He would be his own guardian; two hours every evening women would be free to come to his rooms; there was no telling what the combination of new ideas and new people would do. But all these opportunities seemed tame. They were opportunities offered to him in the normal course of things, not pathways he'd hacked out for himself. There was no tall building he yearned to climb, nor had he desired Jo enough to bed her in the back of the garage.

On the landing Reuben tapped his feet urgently. But Asa wasn't finished with the painting. What had his ancestor

Abbott meant by it? Was it a message, and what was it? He could not, of course, have imagined an Asa to stand before it a generation in the future, pondering his own character; therefore, it was a message for a larger audience.

"Let's *go*," Reuben called. Jerry came out of a room down the hall and stood beside Asa.

"What do you think this painting is about?" Asa asked him.

"About? It's not about anything. It's not a book."

"Aren't paintings about things too?"

"What do *you* think it's about?" When Asa didn't say anything, Jerry continued. "You think it's about you, don't you? You think it's a picture of your genetic heritage, or something like that, right?"

"What? No." Asa had no idea what Jerry meant.

"The Puritan will imposed on New England, the shaping of America—that sort of stuff. Well, it isn't. It's a picture of one of his daughters draped in a sheet, standing in front of a window that looks out on some mountains."

Asa looked at the painting from this point of view; it was exactly what Jerry said. And yet, it was other things too. A pebble hit him on the shoulder.

"Let's get the hell out of here, I'm tired of this place," Reuben said. He had a handful of pebbles and was tossing them at the ceiling. The rope was slung over his shoulder, wrinkling and wriggling every time he raised his arm. "I'm tired. I played a soccer game today. I just want to sack out."

Asa shut his eyes, to have the pleasure of opening them and seeing the angel still there. But Jerry took him by the arm, while his eyes were closed, and turned him toward the stairwell, so that he saw the arched window and Reuben's yellow head, upright this time but silhouetted as it had been when he was falling. There was to be no more dawdling. Asa buttoned his blue coat. On the way out, both to impress Reuben and to keep alive a memory for himself, he snitched a postcard of the painting from the rack on the information desk.

"Why not steal the painting?" Reuben said. "That's not much of a reproduction."

For a minute it seemed like a good idea—that is, an idea Asa could imagine enacting. They could slice it out of its frame and he could roll it up and take it back to Choate in his suitcase. This was how art thieves operated in movies. He desired the painting enough to consider doing it; did that mean Reuben acted on his desires because they were more powerful than Asa's? But what possible desire could he have to break into this museum? Or to steal rugs from out of his neighbor's front hall, or steam open his father's mail, or any of the daring and useless things he did? Perhaps he desired action—any action—and would go to great lengths to provide himself with it. Reuben wanted to make an impression on the world, to leave his footprints all over the snow; Asa wanted to enjoy the snowstorm. No, he was not being accurate, he was letting himself off too easily. He just wanted to get through life, and that was difficult enough without adding the danger of falling off the scaffolding or ending up in juvenile court for larceny.

Just to get through life was no ambition. It was the opposite of ambition. Walking through the leaves with Jerry and Reuben, both yawning, Asa tried to infuse himself with desires and hopes and plans. The night was helpful; dim now, and misty, warming as rainy air moved in, it was an atmosphere of change in which trees and buildings blurred and might be something else, anything. Halloween was coming, and Asa recalled himself as a pirate, a soldier, a ghost (this gave him pause, but he refused to dwell on past ghostliness), knocking on Brattle Street doors. Blackening his upper lip with cork had convinced him of his mustache; a costume was useful in that way—it could catapult you into another life. Would a white silk scarf and different shoes make his life at Harvard dangerous and free?

Asa resolved to do a dangerous thing sometime before going off to college.

Early in April, Parker and Asa were accepted at Harvard. This was no surprise. What was surprising was that Reuben managed to get in as well, and that they were to room together. Jerry would be their fourth. This, and the fact that their rooms were in Weld Hall, an ungainly Victorian folly, rather than in the more distinguished Georgian Holworthy, upset Asa. Weld had the reputation of housing out-of-towners and football players. "We don't belong in there," Asa said. Parker was unsympathetic. "We'll never be in there," he said, "we'll be busy." And then there was the problem of Jerry.

"I don't see what's the matter with him," Parker said.

"He knows too much."

"You mean he's a wonk?"

"No, I think he just knows stuff, without studying. His parents are Communists."

"Hey, terrific. Does he have a beard?"

"He and Reuben kind of shut people out, you know."

"They won't shut us out. Reuben can't shut us out, we're his pals."

Asa wasn't sure of anything. Packing his suitcases in June, taking down his framed photographs of the farm in New Hampshire and himself with father and mother on the Nantucket beach, shaking hands with his teachers, exchanging summer plans with his classmates—a full quarter of whom would be in the Yard with him in September—he brooded on the summer ahead of him, the Last Summer, and how to cement his relations with Reuben, and what bold feat he could achieve.

It was late in June, approaching another midsummer, and they were racing up the coast in Reuben's car. Jo sat in the front seat with her hand on Reuben's naked thigh, Asa and Parker sat in the back, squirming on the sand left over from previous trips. As usual, they had argued about where to go. Asa and Jo wanted to go south, where the sand was fine and the water warm. Parker always took Reuben's side, and Reuben wanted to go north, to Plum Island, because there it was forbidden to swim or picnic. "It's too cold up there," Asa said, "and we're not supposed to swim anyhow." "No crowds," Reuben answered, and blasted out of the circular driveway at forty miles an hour. "Skinny-dipping, herons, no lifeguards—it's paradise." Asa and Jo smoked more than usual in protest.

Each time Jo took out a cigarette Asa leaned forward between the front seats to light it. Sometimes their hands brushed. Then, in reparation, Jo stroked the gold hairs on Reuben's leg more intently. Reuben had become gold all over, like a perfectly done piece of french toast. Jo was brown, dark brown, and the whites of her eyes and her teeth looked like porcelain chips. Parker burned, so he kept a hat on his head and a towel around his neck at all times; nonetheless, his nose was blistered. To protect it, he'd bought a plastic nose cover, which he kept in place with a piece of masking tape. He looked somewhat like a heron with this beaky attachment, which he called "my nib." Reuben now referred to him as His Nibs. Asa found all of this irritating. He did not burn, he did not toast, either. He became ruddied and flushed and looked like a six-year-old who'd spent too long making sandcastles. He put tropical balms all over himself and wished he had a real tan, but he never achieved one until August.

They sped north, weaving from lane to lane because Reuben wanted to break his record from the last trip. They had a cold chicken and a loaf of rye bread and eight hard-boiled eggs packed by Lolly in a hamper. Parker had supplied a six-pack bought by Clem and warming rapidly in the hot car. The hope of a still-cool beer kept Reuben's foot on the accelerator; Parker kept placing his hand on the bottles and yelling, "Faster, faster, it's cooking!"

The road out of the city passed over the Mystic River. From the crest of the bridge Asa could see all of the Charlestown shipyards laid out in a snaking line, with half-built boats—gray destroyers and cargo carriers—fixed in the still, silver water. It was a view he looked forward to. The bridge was high enough to miniaturize the sight, so that it seemed to be a toy industrial center, complete with tiny workers and thin plumes of factory smoke. Reuben had noticed him craning and twisting around to take in the spectacle each time they passed it. On this steamy late-morning ride he chose to comment.

"Some bridge," he said.

Asa shifted his glance up; it was an extraordinary bridge. The lacework of its struts and wires was beautiful in the way a birch forest is beautiful in winter: feathery, spare, seeming to have great depth by virtue of intricacy. "Yes, pretty," he said.

"It's a goddam monument," said Reuben. "Anything this high and complicated is a work of art."

"I was really looking at the shipyard," Asa mumbled.

"Huh?" Reuben said. He passed a few cars. "How's the beer?"

"Hot, hot, hot," said Parker.

At the beach Asa and Parker spread their towels the customary twenty feet away from Reuben and Jo, to leave them in privacy. As payoff for this, Asa and Parker kept the food in their area. Parker dug a hole near the high-water mark and buried the beer. Asa draped Parker's shirt over the hamper and put a rock on top. But the beer never cooled down, the shirt blew off the hamper twice, and the eggs, when unpeeled, were sweating and rubbery. Still, the pleasures of the beach— the simplicity of the horizon, the fresh, tart smell of the sand, the gulls who circled the picnic crying for scraps—put them all in a good mood. After eating, Reuben and Jo retired to their towel, where they stripped and lay in each other's arms for the rest of the afternoon. Sometimes their limbs thrashed a little. Asa tried not to look in their direction.

That was difficult. Parker had a tendency to stare at them and describe what they were doing to Asa, who sat with his back resolutely turned toward them. But the descriptions were tantalizing and incomplete—"Oh wow, she's really . . . boy"—and Asa would crane his head over his shoulder to see for himself. What he saw made him miserable. They were beautiful and naked and in each other's arms and he was hot, stupid from beer, and alone. He wished he could tap Reuben on the shoulder and cut in, replace him as Jo's partner as simply as he might at a dance.

Could he steal Jo away with cigarettes and subtle touches? After all, she had kissed him. That would be a dangerous project. Why had she kissed him? He pretended to look down the beach and watched, for a moment, the star shape they had made of themselves on the red towel. Reuben lay sideways on top of Jo reading a comic book; she was staring up at the sky. One breast pointed toward Asa. The day was very hot, and their images wiggled before Asa's eyes, as if they were melting. He turned toward the sea, which was also

quivering. At the horizon a band of dancing molecules confused the border between water and air. There was a melting
boat—or was it a gull? Maybe only a wave cresting on a
sandbar. The shape of everything began to change. Even his
own feet, where he rested his eyes for relief, were huge and
pulsing and nacreous in the heat. It had been nearly a year
since she'd kissed him. She might not remember doing it.
But didn't the fact of it guarantee him some sort of access to
her? He peeked over at them again. Reuben had shifted and
now lay blocking Jo's body with his own. One of his legs
enclosed both of hers, his weight was on his elbow, his hand
was on her belly. Some of her thick, salt-curled hair was
caught in the crook of his arm.

Asa drank another beer. The sun got lower and hotter.
Parker, who'd been asleep, woke and said, "Let's go swimming." But the water was cold. It curled their toes and made
their heads hurt. Parker ran in yelling "Here I go!" and shot
up from the water almost instantly. Asa watched from shore.
"Too damned cold," said Parker, resuming his nib, hat, and
towel. Then the wind shifted and some flies arrived. Asa
placed an egg at the edge of the towel to distract them, but
they wanted blood. The trick was to kill them in midbite,
when for a moment they were still. After six bites and two
deaths, Asa was ready to leave. They didn't bite Parker. "They
don't like my smell," he said. "You are just what they like."
There was a cloud of them above Asa's head, humming.

"Let's go," he called toward the red towel.

"Not yet," Reuben called back.

"There are *flies*," Asa insisted.

"Not over here."

"I'm coming over with them." Asa stood up and walked
toward them with his halo. Jo turned onto her belly for mod-
esty. A fly settled on her ass.

"All right," she said. There was a flat, dark welt on her buttock. "Let's go."

They left the uneaten eggs in a row on the sand. Reuben forgot his comic book, Jo forgot her watch ("Good," she said in the car, "I want a new one, with Roman numerals"), Asa forgot the brass-handled bottle opener he'd remembered to take from the lowboy at the last minute that morning, and Parker forgot his shirt. Before the low, white car had reached the edge of Boston, these objects had been washed over by the ocean and changed. The comic book swelled with water, the watch stopped, the shirt ripped and curled into a ball, the brass took on the green cast of the sea. Gulls poked the eggs with their beaks and tattered them. Sand and tide crept up on these things, and by ruining them made them mysterious. To the next visitors, the next afternoon, they would be not debris but artifacts, visible memories. "Look, an old picnic. There was a woman with this watch, and they were drinking . . ." And that couple's afternoon would be enlarged to include all the other summer afternoons when people had warmed their water-cold feet in the sand and looked across the waves to see—couldn't you, just over the horizon, see it?—Spain.

The ride back was punctuated by realizations of loss: "My watch!" "My shirt!" "Shit, my comic," "Oh God, mother's brass thing." Only Jo was pleased. Reuben complained most, though his loss was the easiest to rectify. "I hadn't finished it," he groaned. "You can get another with a nickel," Jo said. "Too cheap?" "I just wanted to finish it." Asa decided the best approach with his mother was to announce having lost the bottle opener immediately and be contrite. Parker was planning to buy a pink shirt—maybe two—at J. August on Monday. Jo wanted to go directly to Shreve's for her watch, but nobody else wanted to. Asa and Parker got a chance to see her work on Reuben. "It wouldn't take fifteen minutes," she said, stroking his arm that stretched to the steering wheel. "I know just the one I want. We could just run in—we could double-park and leave them in the car." She tilted her head back to indicate "them." Reuben stared at the road. She began to stroke his upper thigh, and once or twice her fingers dipped into the dark above the edge of his shorts. Reuben smiled but said nothing. Then he took her hand, rather roughly, and placed it in her lap. "Forget it," he said. He turned his face toward her, smiling and remote. "Go with your daddy."

Although Asa was surprised by Reuben's coldness and un-susceptibility (what wouldn't he, Asa, do to have Jo's fingers walking up and down his thigh?), he also felt a sympathetic dislike of her and an urge to torment her. Jo would be grat-ifying to hurt because she was tough and beautiful and ex-pected to be treated well. He could sense Reuben's pleasure in denying her, and wondered if they didn't both take delight in his meanness—he for the simple power of it, she for the novelty. How long, Asa wondered, would it be before he was sure enough of himself to be mean rather than abject with women? It might never happen. He couldn't imagine being anything but accommodating to a girl he was crazy about. More evidence of his weakness, or, from another point of view, his good upbringing.

They had come to the bridge again. The fat, four o'clock June sun was lighting up the structure, making a net that caught Asa's attention. He looked at it, rather than the scene it encircled, and saw it as a "monument," as Reuben saw it. Under their tires the steel rang and quivered—the bridge was a vibrating corridor between country and city. Asa was struck by an awareness of progress through a landscape, as if for the first time he understood what travel was: He moved and things stayed behind. Yet that description was not exactly right, and he let his head fall back against the cushions open-eyed, so the scaffolding of the bridge could strum his vision and, perhaps, provoke a better explanation. Everything was shiny and hot and changing, everything was moving past him—he reversed his understanding: He was the same, an open eye, and the world shifted and shone. And these thoughts themselves flashed through his mind the way the changing scene flashed past his eye; for a moment each was entire and round, then had gone and was unimaginable, or rather lived only in the imagination because it was not present. But where was he in this landscape? Only an eye, either moving or static? He remembered his resolve to Do Something. But it was hot, the car smelled comfortably of cigarettes and suntan oil, and the world flickering beyond the windows could be a roll of pictures unfurled for his pleasure—Reuben pulled the car over abruptly and got out.

"Hey," said Parker.

"Checking out this bridge," said Reuben. He put his hand on one of the girders (it was almost too large for his palm to fit around) and leaned on it.

Asa sank into a stupor. He knew what was coming: Reuben saying, Who's going to climb this bridge with me? He could hear himself volunteering, to placate his ambitions. He could hear Jo's protests, or encouragement, it didn't make any difference because she was irrelevant to bridge climbing. Parker stepped out of the car also, and stood beside Reuben on the grillwork of the walkway, assessing the possible approaches they could take. Asa stayed in the backseat and thought about how he was too cowardly to refuse to climb and too cowardly to enjoy what he would agree to do. Then he stopped thinking about it. He said, "Yes, sure," and decided it would be like a trip to the dentist—he would determine to live through it nobly. His objective was to endure.

But he knew that objective made the enterprise a failure. What he did might fool Parker, and even Reuben, into thinking he was brave, but he wouldn't be brave, he would be acting brave. He was out of alignment somehow—and when had he not been? Bicycling around sleeping Cambridge, but what sort of adventure was that? When Jo had kissed him and he'd asked her to kiss him again: That had been the intersection of desire and action. But it hadn't worked. She'd gone back into the garage.

"Great bridge, I've wanted to climb it for years," Reuben said, settling himself at the steering wheel. "We'll go Monday night. Thayer, you're not going to fink out, are you?"

Asa could say yes and grow up in a hurry, discard his friends with one word, and put pranks and daredeviltry behind him. He realized it would mean that. The pressure of having to reaffirm popped the shell of the situation; the inside, the foolishness and foolhardiness, was exposed. He realized there was a choice, and he wanted summer, risk, admiration—all waiting for him on the struts of that bridge. Climbing the bridge was the closest he could come to being Reuben, and wasn't that his real ambition? He wanted that the way Reuben wanted to be high and perilous.

"No, no," he said urgently, "I won't fink out."

On Monday morning Reuben phoned to say he should wear sneakers, long pants, and a long-sleeved shirt. "And wear dark colors, so they don't notice us." They were to meet at the Solas' at eight; Roberto was going along. "Should I bring some rope?" Asa asked. Reuben laughed and said they weren't going to use rope. "That's cheating," he said, and hung up.

Asa mowed the back and front lawns without being asked, oiled the lawn mower, and sanded the rust off his bicycle. At four in the afternoon he thought he might die before the sun went down. He lay on his mahogany bed and stared at the ceiling and wished he could sleep, and oversleep, to wake at ten o'clock when the crickets were singing and his friends had reached the halfway point on those thick wires. For a while he did sleep, and dreamed he was kissing Jo, lying in the hollow of a dune. He woke up sweating and empty-headed, feeling he had passed through danger. Flies bombarded his screen, the late sun fell on his naked feet, and he was conscious of summer, the slowness, the roundness of it. From far below he heard the faint rattle of his mother making dinner. He stretched. In the middle of stretching, just at the point when his muscles were about to tingle with relief and pleasure, he remembered the climb; a pain went through him, and in his mouth was a bath of penny-flavored saliva. The clock in the hall bonged six. He got up and put on a navy-blue sweatshirt.

The Solas were eating dessert when he arrived. Professor Sola sat at the middle of their long, polished table with a son at either end. Each had a bowl of cream with strawberries bobbing in it. Reuben had a cream mustache. Asa was deposited in the chair opposite Professor Sola by Lolly, who then brought a bowl for him too.

"What are your plans for tonight, boys?"

"Midnight ride," Reuben said.

"Sultry. Are these the dog days?"

"No, Papa, those are in August," Reuben said. "Why don't you swim?"

"Perhaps." He pushed his spoon around, trying to gather more cream. "I'll have coffee," he said, quietly. Lolly appeared immediately with a cup. "Will you have some?" He smiled at Asa.

"Thank you." Again the instantaneous appearance of a cup,

as though Lolly were a mind reader. Reuben and Roberto were not drinking coffee.

"A cognac?" asked Professor Sola.

Reuben started laughing. "Papa, it's Asa," he said.

"No reason not to be hospitable."

Reuben slumped in his chair, and Asa felt something banging at his ankle. It was Reuben's foot, warning him not to accept cognac.

"No, thank you, sir," he said obediently.

"No cognac?" Professor Sola was nearly awakened by this. "Remarkable. If I were to offer it to my children, I can't imagine them refusing."

"You never do," Roberto said.

"It's too hot for cognac," said Professor Sola. "So, you will go on a midnight ride. Where will you go?"

"Oh, somewhere cool," Reuben said, airily. "The beach or something."

"Summer nights," Professor Sola muttered. "Summer nights." Then he looked at Asa. "What is your field?"

"I don't know yet, sir. We won't have to decide until sophomore year."

"But you must have an inclination. A tendency. Even Reuben has that—a tendency to daydream. So he will probably major in art history. That's an excellent field for a dreamer. And Roberto"—he leaned his head slightly to the left, where Roberto sat; Roberto shut his eyes—"if and when he reaches college, will probably major in rebellion and criticizing his betters, or, as it's called these days, political science. But you strike me as more contemplative than rebellious. And contemplative is not the same as dreamy. Perhaps mathematics? That's a contemplative science."

"No, sir, I can't do calculus."

"Botany?"

"I think English literature," Asa said.

"Pah," said Professor Sola. Asa flinched. "That's for women." This was astonishing, because Professor Sola taught English literature. "It's the refuge of those who can't think," he continued. "Botany. Quiet, orderly, elegant. Consider botany, Asa."

"But sir, there must have been some reason that you chose English literature."

"It was different," he said. He said nothing else, so Asa was left wondering if English had been different once, or if Professor Sola's case was different from his own.

He tried again. "I love to read."

"Then for God's sake major in botany. If you enroll in my department, every book you've loved you will learn to hate; and by the end of two years you will have become an illiterate. It is only useful if you begin as an illiterate, such as Roberto."

"What good is it then, having an inclination?" Asa asked.

The bell rang. "That's Parker," said Reuben, rising.

"Lolly will answer it. We're not finished with dinner." Professor Sola swirled the dregs in his coffee cup and looked into it; he seemed disappointed and put the cup back on its saucer.

Parker came in, got strawberries, told Professor Sola he intended to major in French. "Why not Russian?" he was asked.

"Baudelaire didn't write in Russian."

This answer started Asa giggling. Professor Sola politely pretended not to notice and continued his conversation with Parker in counterpoint to Asa's muffled gasps.

"Tolstoy wrote in Russian."

"Rimbaud didn't write in Russian."

"All the French speak English; why learn French?"

"All Americans speak only English. I think it's impolite."

"And Pushkin."

"I've read him in English."

Asa stood up and headed for the bathroom in the hall, where he could let himself laugh. It was the image of Baudelaire in an enormous, bulky Russian coat made of weasel or fox, striding down the green boulevards, smelling of herring, mooning over his melancholy, that had done him in. He pounded his hand on the wall beside the sink and looked at himself in the little mirror. There were tears in his eyes. He realized he was probably hysterical. Somebody ought to come and slap him on the cheeks to calm him down. He put his head under the faucet and ran cold water on his face.

"Are you okay?" Reuben asked. He was standing in the hallway, looking at Asa through the half-open door.

"Fine. Wasn't that a funny conversation, though? Wasn't the idea of Baudelaire in a big coat—" Asa sputtered and drops of water flew off his cheeks.

"Cut it out," Reuben said. "You don't have to come."

"That isn't *it*."

"You don't want to. Why don't you stay here and talk to Papa about books?"

"You think I'm chicken."

"He'll give you some brandy, he'll show you his dirty etchings, you'll have a great time." Reuben leaned against the wall with one shoulder, crossed his arms, and smiled. "It's more your style."

Asa began to cry; his throat got bigger than his neck, his back and shoulders shook independently of the rest of his body, which he held straight and rigid. One hot tear contrasted on his skin with the cold water; the rest he suppressed. Reuben put a hand on his wiggling arm.

"You're not going to fool anybody by coming. You'll just be a liability."

"Terrific," Asa whispered. He didn't trust his throat enough to speak.

"Jesus," Reuben said, turning away. "I don't give a damn. Don't do it for *me*."

"Why not?" A few more tears got out. Asa drank them. "Why not?" he repeated.

"Look, Asa. We're pals." Reuben was facing him again. "I know what you're like. We're not the same—but we're pals. Okay? Okay?"

"You mean it?"

"Yes."

"Well, then, what have I been—" Asa stopped.

"Trying to prove? Is that what you mean? I don't know, Thayer. Peer pressure."

Asa sniffed and wiped his cheeks. Reuben had retreated again and was smiling in his usual chilly way. "Stop sniveling," he said. "We're going now."

Reuben went back into the dining room. Asa could hear the chairs scraping the floor as Roberto and Parker stood up. He blew his nose and went in there also. Everyone was standing except Professor Sola, who had started on a second cup of coffee.

"We're off, Papa," said Reuben.

"Yes, boys. Be back by midnight." He laughed, and so did his sons.

"And entertain Asa."

"Asa's not coming?" asked Parker, addressing Reuben. Asa stood behind his chair. They could all hear the early crickets.

"Asa's not coming," said Reuben.

The screen door at the back of the house banged three times, the Porsche's motor made its small explosions in the night, and they were gone. Asa stood behind his chair listening to the silence they had left, which was unbroken by Professor Sola. He felt tired, and old, and sat down again.

"What are they really going to do?" asked Reuben's father, suddenly.

"Climb the Mystic River Bridge."

"Yes." He sighed. "You are a brave young man," he told Asa. "Have a cognac." Lolly appeared with two glasses. "Here's to . . ." He held his glass up and looked at Asa, but didn't say anything.

"What, sir?"

"Here's to History," concluded Professor Sola, after a long pause. "We'll all be part of it sooner or later."

When at ten-thirty the car turned into the driveway again, Asa and Professor Sola were on the sofa, bent over a folder of Picasso's erotic drawings, just as Reuben had predicted. The air conditioner muffled the sound of tires on gravel and the screen door, which banged twice. So Parker and Roberto, materializing out of nowhere in the study whose atmosphere was gilded by the amber-glass lamps that hung from the bookshelves, startled the pair. Professor Sola recovered himself quickly, but Asa had seen a horrible expression fix itself briefly on his face—open eyes, open mouth, eyebrows climbing to his hairline. He clenched his teeth (the Sola sound of grinding competed for a moment with the hum of machinery) and put his face in order.

"Professor Sola—" Parker said.

"Papa—" Roberto broke in.

Asa felt the cold air streaming unpleasantly past his head. Parker's sleeves were torn, he noticed, and Roberto's pants were damp and spotted with mud.

"Reuben fell," Roberto said. "He fell off. We tried, we

couldn't, we looked, we didn't see." He was speaking in bursts, but flatly, each phrase an uninflected exhalation. He sat down in an armchair, but still he kept talking, or what seemed to him to be talking. "We thought maybe, but it wasn't, there weren't any rocks, and we tried on the shore, I didn't see, we heard that splash."

"Enough," said his father. "That's enough now."

"I've called the Coast Guard," said Parker. "I'm going back. They're going to drag the river. I'm going back." He turned toward Asa, fierce. "You should have been there," he said. "You belonged there."

Asa was cold. The book, with its sporting couples and beribboned dogs and centaurs, lay open on his lap. He was aware of his toes wiggling inside his sneakers, of Professor Sola's cigarette burning untended in the marble ashtray. The phone rang. Nobody answered it. Roberto started up again: "It wasn't easy, we didn't notice until, there was so much garbage in the river, I never imagined—because it was pretty straightforward."

At that, his father began to laugh. "Pretty straightforward! As a climb, you mean? It wasn't much of a challenge, you mean that? You can't understand how it happened, because Reuben kept saying how it wasn't very difficult? Do you mean that?" He sat up and opened his eyes wide. "Do you, Roberto?"

"Oh, Papa," Roberto said. He sounded tired and resigned.

"When she jumped—" Professor Sola said. Asa came out of his daze. But Roberto interrupted.

"No, no. It wasn't—he was never like you, never."

"Me? I'm not talking about myself."

"You plural, you together, you who weren't brave enough to live, that's who," Roberto said.

"And what do you know about bravery?" said Professor Sola, softly, shutting his eyes.

"I'm going back there," Parker said. "I'm taking the car. Are you coming?" He looked at Asa. Asa shook his head.

"I'm coming," said Professor Sola.

The river was dragged until one in the morning and the whole of Tuesday as well. Professor Sola sat on the bank in his black suit and watched. Tuesday evening he called Parker and asked him to arrange a memorial service—"Get in touch with his friends. We'll never have a body." Thursday at midday a hundred and fifty young men and women gathered in the Solas' living room, rarely used, where they heard a string quartet by Mozart and a speech on youth by a junior-faculty history teacher at Andover. Professor Sola did not attend. Housman's "To an Athlete Dying Young" was read, and Jerry Kuhn, who'd flown up from New York and seated himself beside Asa, who still felt cold, leaned close to him and whispered, "I knew they'd do that. I knew it." Jo wore bleached linen; she had cut most of her hair off and her unsuntanned neck rose up from her collar like a white pillar. When it was over everybody left quickly. Professor Sola had decided that the pool needed to be repainted and was having it drained; he was overseeing the workmen during the service. Jerry, who'd caught a glimpse of this scene as he left the house in Asa's wake, said, "Does he think he'll find Reuben at the bottom of that body of water?" Asa dragged his bicycle out of its spot in the bushes without answering and rode all the way to Walden Pond for a swim.

It was late in June when Reuben died. Asa caught a cold and stayed in bed reading Sherlock Holmes until a few days before the Fourth of July. Parker called once, to see if he wanted to go to the beach; Asa said no, and Parker didn't call again. On July 3, Asa put himself on a bus going north to spend some weeks with his grandparents in New Hampshire. He did not drive into town with them to see the fireworks, although this had been one of his favorite events when he was a boy. He stayed home, blowing his nose and reading Maupassant's short stories, which comforted him with their predictability. He was asleep; even his limbs were asleep, and tingled every time he tried to move them. He woke up briefly at the start of August, when he decided to return to Cambridge. When he got there, he had fallen asleep again. Although it had been easier to cease functioning with his grandparents, who were indulgent and didn't expect him to do anything more than gather some eggs for breakfast, he was too tired to go back, or go anywhere else. He mowed the lawn, he polished the silver, he ran errands for his father, he did his own laundry. Now and then he surfaced—it was as though he lived underwater, what with the remnants of his cold and the dearth of sensation or emotion—and looked at the calendar. August 29, September 2: He wouldn't have been surprised to see June on the page and find himself living the whole of the blank and chilly summer over again.

Eventually it was time to register. The authorities had decided, perhaps out of sympathy, to leave Parker, Asa, and Jerry alone in their four-room suite. Roberto was back at Manter Hall for another year of cramming; he took over the empty room as a storage space for the growing pile of stolen objects he was accumulating. While Parker and Asa were unpacking new tweed suits and old Shetland sweaters, Roberto was unfolding Oriental rugs of mysterious provenance and putting first editions of Hemingway into bureau drawers. "Art collecting seems to run in the family, one way or another," Jerry said to Asa.

Asa refused to speak to Jerry, and Parker refused to speak

to Asa. Asa couldn't forgive the comment about Professor Sola and the pool; Parker couldn't forgive Asa's absence at the bridge. Inevitably an alliance developed between Parker and Jerry. They did Baudelaire together (that was how Asa thought of it), speaking French, wearing European-style shirts without buttons on the collar, replaying all the banal conversations they'd overheard in the Union, and spoofing their classmates.

Asa didn't want a friend. He was thinking of concentrating in art history, with a minor in English, or perhaps the other way around. He was taking an intimate slide-lecture course on the history of Western art at the Fogg. Every Tuesday afternoon, from three to five-thirty, he sat in the dark, dusty-smelling basement auditorium and was lulled by a succession of beautiful, colored images looming at the end of the room. There were about fifteen other students, half of them Radcliffe girls; these contrived to bump against him as they went in and out of class. He didn't pay attention.

One November afternoon, in the middle of Greek vases, there flashed onto the screen a painting, startling in its color and scope by contrast with the ebony and umber of the terracottas, which they'd been looking at for two weeks. "Icarus," said the professor, "as he was seen a thousand years later. How insignificant he is here. You can barely distinguish him." The pointer moved to a ripple in the water, bisected by two little legs. "It's the peasant and the land that are dominant." And Asa looked. Yes, in the corner, the flurry of drowning, while all around the world hummed and plowed and trod between its furrows. His face got hot and his palms began to sweat. Nobody had noticed—that he was crying, that Icarus was dying. He kept crying and getting hotter, as if the cold that had clamped onto him in the Solas' study had finally let go, and he were now thawing. All that had been was changed, all the world was different, there weren't any heroes, there weren't any summers at the pool to come, there weren't any myths—Asa's litany of loss, first enunciated in that basement, became a train of thought he carried everywhere. Down the street to romantic poetry at Seaver Hall, accompanied by his inner chant: No more myths, no more summer; into the Union, filling his tray with meat loaf and custard: Everything is changed, everything is gone. Eventually he got used to it, it was a familiar part of the landscape, this voice that never stopped. He bought a print of Breughel's painting from the Fogg and hung it on the wall opposite his bed. He stopped going to the museum course; he had gotten what he needed from it.

Asa graduated in 1960 in English, without honors. He and Jerry had resumed relations in the middle of junior year and were going to Paris together to get jobs at the *Herald Tribune*. Parker had drifted into club life, had written for the *Lampoon* and given black-tie dinners in his Eliot House rooms, to which he always invited Jerry (who wouldn't go because of Parker's friends' anti-Semitism) and never invited Asa (who would have welcomed a touch of the high life). To their surprise Parker got a *summa* in history and went straight into graduate school, where he distinguished himself while Asa and Jerry ate tripe and suffered grievous stomach pains. The grim Paris autumn sent Asa back to America and a stopgap job reading novel manuscripts at Little, Brown. They were terrible, but unlike most of the readers, he wasn't convinced he could write a better one. What had he got to write about? Within three years Jerry was ensconced at a rewrite desk near the Champs-Élysées, Parker had a job waiting for him at Yale when he finished his thesis, and Asa was learning book production—riffling through pages without reading them to count the lines, poring over type catalogues, making deals with paper suppliers.

And by then Roberto had vanished. He was to turn up periodically, always enthusiastic about a new project. Desalinization of Cape Cod Bay was one; for several years he worried about the water table on the Eastern seaboard. Then he got a job at Sotheby's in London, but that didn't last long because there was some trouble about the disappearance of a Bernini plaster study for an angel. He was against bomb shelters and for disarmament, and circulated a newsletter on these issues for a year or two; Asa always got a copy. After a long period of silence he resurfaced, having become a documentary filmmaker specializing in Latin America. Sometimes he appeared in Cambridge with a new car and a beautiful, sleek woman, took Asa—later Asa and Fay—out to dinner at the Ritz and told incredible stories about his life. Other times he came alone, in Reuben's Porsche, getting on for a decade old, and sat in Asa's living room drinking rum and brooding. He stayed in touch with Asa because Asa stayed in touch with Professor Sola, and Roberto had, in his words, "divested" himself of the family. "What's left of it to divest," he added. But he wanted the news.

The news wasn't good. Professor Sola had had a throat cancer and now whispered and wheezed his infrequent sentences. He rarely saw anyone except Asa, who had started visiting while he was at Harvard out of desperation and continued visiting out of duty. The professor spent most of his time in his study with the amber lights on, making a catalogue of his art holdings; these had been increased by Roberto's hoard, which had been abandoned by Roberto and presented by Asa to the father as recompense for losing his other son. Roberto had disappeared when Asa was a sophomore and still dependent on Professor Sola's company. He went there every

Friday night for dinner and listened to rambling monologues about Rembrandt, Germany in the twenties, the Harvard English faculty, and the problems of the pool.

"You know, it only alienated my neighbors more when I built the pool. They thought it was the height of ostentation. I was prepared to invite them all, to consider it their pool as well. They didn't want it in the vicinity."

"Why alienated them more? What had alienated them to begin with?" Asa asked. He had learned that Professor Sola, unlike Reuben, didn't mind being asked direct questions.

"Oh, why does anybody dislike the Jews? I never knew."

"It was that?"

"Maybe." The old man said nothing else, and Asa felt unsatisfied, for once.

He found out, too late to make any difference, all that he'd wanted to know about Reuben's mother. Blonde and rich, she'd passed for Aryan, supplied her husband and infant (Roberto; Reuben had been born in America) with food, obtained passports for the family and gotten them out of Germany, and killed herself five years later. "Why not?" Professor Sola had said, telling this story one long summer evening. "What was the point of her life after that? She'd saved the people she cared about, given me two children, compromised her identity, abandoned her country. Her work was done."

"Did you feel the same?"

"Did I want to die? Well, yes, but she died first, and there were the boys, so I stayed."

Asa never forgot his saying "stayed," as though the world were a place, like Boston or Paris, and there were other places to be.

"And what was her name?"

"Marthe. Martha."

So Grace remained a mystery. It was a mystery Asa pondered by himself in his living room late at night, after Roberto had come and gone, or anytime he felt adrift or startled by some memory of the past. He avoided the Solas' end of Brattle Street, driving down Mount Auburn to get to his parents' house on Sundays when he and Fay went there for dinner. He braved that five-pronged intersection only when he intended to visit Professor Sola.

And at the end of the sixties, Professor Sola died. His cancer had recurred, and he told Asa he didn't intend to have it treated. Asa wrote to Roberto, care of General Delivery, Hollywood; the letter returned after two weeks, addressee unknown. He put a few ads in the movie trade journals, called Parker at Yale, but Roberto was untraceable. There was a strange funeral at the Mount Auburn Cemetery with Asa and Fay and their baby girl, two cadaverous professors emeritus of English, and Lolly. Lolly had arranged the service, which consisted of a Unitarian minister reading Psalms. Reuben's marker was on the left, Marthe's on the right.

Roberto turned up several weeks later, drank rum, listened to the news, and talked about home computers, which he claimed were the wave of the future. Never, in all those years, in all those evenings Asa spent with Roberto or his father, did any of them say Reuben's name.

After Professor Sola was dead, Asa unrolled the Breughel print, which he'd kept in the back of the off-season clothes closet in the guest room, and tacked it above his desk, which stood in a corner of the living room. Fay didn't like it. "I think that's an ugly painting," she said more than once. "It's depressing, that's what."

"Oh, I don't think so," said Asa. "It's about how life goes on, you know?" But he used it to get depressed with. During the day, or when there were people in the room, he never looked at it. At night, after Fay, tired from the baby, went to sleep at nine, he'd sit on the sofa, and stare at the plowman, the hillside, the feeble effort of Icarus not to drown, and drink his scotch, and—what? He described it to himself as "remembering." But he avoided specific memories. He drifted around in the past, smelling the roses that studded the Solas' garage, seeing again the finely turned column of Jo's arm, tasting the chlorine in his throat from too many dives into the pool. Occasionally he tasted real tears. And sometimes he heard his old litany: No more summer, no more myths— but it was halting and faint and had lost its power to hypnotize. Because life did go on, he and Fay had bought a shack on the Cape and had their own summers now. So what was he lacking, and what was he crying for?

Quite simply, the best love he'd ever known.

THE DISCREPANCIES

W hat Asa had said to me was, "I had a boyhood friend who died." This was in passing, in the middle of a conversation about friendship. "Who?" I asked.

"Oh, he's dead."

"I know."

"His name was Reuben. He had an accident."

"When was this? What kind of accident?"

"Oh, it was ages ago. We were teenagers. He was climbing something and he fell."

"What?"

"What?"

"What was he climbing?" Sometimes conversation with Asa was impossible. He would retreat into stupidity and I would have to spell everything out for him.

"He was climbing the Mystic River Bridge. What do you want to know all this for?"

"Don't you want to know things about me and my life?"

"Sure." And his face settled into the expression of lust that he thought was affection. He was capable of affectionate feelings, but these produced a worried expression, as though it hurt to feel them. "I want to know everything." He put his hand on the back of my thigh and slid it down to the dip behind my knee. We were in his office; in a week he was going to be forty-two. He didn't want to know anything about me except how my breasts fit into his palms. We were still in the kissing stage.

"So?" I said.

"Huh?" He had gone behind his cloud. Was it purposeful or inadvertent? Maybe he was hung over. I examined his enormous eyes: bloodshot, but that wasn't unusual. Still, they were puffy underneath and he smelled of witch hazel, which, being slightly alcoholic, gave me the impression of booze by association.

"Are you asleep? Tell me the story."

"I was up too late," he said. This was his euphemism for having drunk too much the night before. He picked up a pencil and pressed the eraser to his lips. He had a habit of caressing inanimate objects in my presence. He would fondle his ruler, stroking it up and down, press paper clips to his cheeks, tap himself on the head with his magnifying glass. I enjoyed his displacement; it was I he wanted to press to his flesh. A year later I was reduced to being jealous of his tools. "You kiss the ruler but you won't kiss me!" I said to him three weeks before I left my job. "Oh, for God's sake," he responded.

But this day, when he put his pencil to his mouth, I was bold and we were enough in love so that when I moved it and put my lips there instead, he kissed me back. The pencil fell on the floor. I tasted him—shaving soap at the corners of his mouth, his coffee, his Lucky—and sighed. He sighed too. It was morning; hours would have to pass before we held each other.

"So what happened?"

"He was a daredevil. Very good-looking, one of those boys who's the natural leader of the group. I worshiped him—I guess." The pencil, retrieved, was tapped on his chin while he pondered whether he had, actually, worshiped. "He was Jewish," Asa said, looking sidelong at me.

"Did he look it?" I asked.

"What's that mean?"

"Joke," I said. "Go on."

"He was an extremist, always pushing himself. Anyhow,

he was doing this crazy thing, climbing this bridge, and he fell off."

"Were you there?"

"No. I chickened out at the last minute and stayed home looking at pornographic art with his father. His father had a hell of an art collection."

"What was he like?"

"Who?"

"Reuben." I kicked the leg of his desk.

"Oh, I don't know. We were such kids. He wasn't a very nice person, I suppose. I don't know if I'd like him now."

"But you liked him then?"

"I was crazy about him," he said. He said it with the same tone he used to say "You're a marvel," or "You're extraordinary," or any of the other things he murmured to me at odd moments passing me in the hall.

"What wasn't nice about him?"

"I think he was manipulative. Also, I think he was immoral. Amoral? Which do I mean?"

"How do I know?" He was always asking me what he meant. "Immoral means evil. Amoral means lacking a sense of right and wrong."

"Amoral. That's just what he was."

Then his phone rang and I went back to my office. It took months for me to extract that story from him. And there's a lot he never told me. I had to extrapolate and invent. When he said, "Then we went on some cockamamie break-in to the museum because Jerry wanted to look at a painting," I had to supply the painting, the pebbles on the roof, the state of his mind.

I don't know why it fascinated me so much, this story he wouldn't tell me. Maybe just because I was jealous of Reuben.

Reuben was part of Asa's mythology—he may have been Asa's mythology in its entirety. When Asa spoke of him his voice was sad, but his face was aglow with the memory of events that had shaped his character and colored his life. What I wanted to know was how that had happened and what, precisely, had happened. I was able to piece together some of the events, but that was only half of it.

Whatever Reuben had meant to Asa, I was sure of one thing: He had planted a seed that had come to blossom only with me. Twenty-five years of dormancy. When I'd met Asa, when he'd leaned over my desk and perfumed my environment, he'd been asleep. I woke him up. That was what I intended to do and I did it. Then I began to see that what happened between us was the duplication of something that had happened long before. Like the past it was nipped in the bud, but it was Asa nipping, not Fate.

Asa had certain predictions about the course of love. They had to come true or he would be adrift. It was the same for me—but my predictions were entirely different. When I looked at him I predicted that we would lie in each other's arms or I would die. I was right. He, on the other hand, predicted that after we lay in each other's arms, our love would die. He was right too, about himself. And he believed this because of Reuben.

I wish I'd known I was just the reincarnation of a bad blond boy, a method of completing a fantasy he had no desire to make into an abiding reality. "This is an interlude, dear," he said to me early on. I didn't listen. I didn't want to know anything about him that didn't fit into my predictions. I kept myself in the dark.

Paradoxically, my very misconception of Asa was my safety. I could retreat into misinterpretations of things he'd said to me, comforting readings of looks he'd given me. The idea that he'd ever loved me was astonishing enough to override any new astonishing information, such as that for the fifth day in a row he would not be coming over after work to make love on the sofa or, if he was daring enough, the bed. The bed was reserved for lunchtime. On the sofa, at five-thirty, he could tell himself he'd been carried away; walking all the way to the bedroom was too premeditated for the evening visit. So he would not be coming, hadn't come yesterday, most likely wouldn't come tomorrow—what did I care? I remembered when he'd come every day.

What I never considered was how things had changed. I didn't want to think about what had happened between May, when the sight of me was enough to take his breath away (I'd heard him gasp when I walked into his office), and November, when the illness of his dogs, the social obligations imposed on him by Fay (Chamber of Commerce dinners, third cousins for cocktails), or simply his own bad temper fortuitously occupied him between five and six-thirty from Monday to Friday.

The truth was that from the moment we'd become lovers he'd stopped loving me. And it was that specific—we'd "done almost everything" on my sofa during the course of our first spring without diminishing his feelings. On the contrary, the more we poked and prodded each other through and around our clothing, the more entranced he became. We developed techniques for producing orgasm through kissing alone and would torment and satisfy each other this way. I don't know how we did it. It had something to do with anticipation and denial, no doubt, but it was also a genuine method. Irreproducible; even with Asa, it never worked after we'd been to bed.

After we lay down, everything became topsy-turvy. In private he was my lover. In public he was wearing a blue shirt and a dark-blue tie and talking on the phone. We would rise up from bed in the early afternoon and eat lunch in the sunshine and discuss, as lovers do, our favorite pastimes. "I think I like being on the bottom," he'd say. Fifteen minutes later, passing me in the hall at work, he wouldn't even look at me. Who was he aiming to fool if not himself? Everybody at the office was accustomed to our glances. This sudden sobriety between us was more noticeable, and more of an announcement, than an increase in flirtation would have been.

How deeply I didn't understand him! On no information at all, I had decided that sex would bind us together. I thought that for a man like that to take off his tie and his shirt and put his body against mine would be so startling that we would share an extraordinary secret: the private world where he was naked and delighted. I would be a witness to the discarding of all his formality. I thought that the passion permitted by his dropping his clothes on the floor would be equal to the formality of the clothes. I was right, but I didn't think it through. I didn't see that once the clothes were on him again, the passion, like a garment with a particular purpose, would be folded away until the next time.

When we were still only kissers and not, technically, lovers, he would touch me in his office, in my office, in the twists and turns of the mahogany staircase. He was as foolish and reckless as I was. It seemed I had opened him up with touch. And I admit I was disappointed to find him so easily reached. Was he just a sensualist whose soul could be tapped by a finger on his cheek? I wanted to capture the heart of a man whose heart was buried deep; what glory in a prize available to anyone with soft hands?

After we became lovers my disappointment faded. He was again the Unapproachable. His foolishness of the kissing months was gone; he retreated into the stiffness that had challenged me originally. I looked at him walking down the hall and tried to remember him in my arms. It was like trying to resolve the two images of a binocular incorrectly positioned for my eyes. And the unlikeliness of those two truths coexisting, along with the surety that they did, was my deepest happiness. He was unhavable—and he was mine.

What made Asa love me was my capacity for inventing him. I conjured up an idea of him that was an idol we both could worship. I had enough information to imagine him, unerringly, as the person he had wished to be twenty years before. If he was silent it was because his thoughts were too complicated to express; if he grumped around the office it was because he knew life ought to be better than life currently was. By reacting to his hidden emotions, I convinced the two of us of the depth of his deepness and the heat of his heat.

I wasn't wrong about him. If I'd been wrong he would never have loved me. But I wasn't exactly right, either. I was off the track in thinking he was as he desired to be. He genuinely wanted passion and danger—from himself and from life—but he had neither. My presuming the existence of his fantasy self made life difficult. For a while he played along with it, but in the end he had to admit it was hopeless. I didn't want to hear it. I wanted my blood-red Yankee. He just wanted peace. He wanted to stop living in somebody else's fantasy, forgetting that it had been his as well.

That's what I don't forgive. I could never have imagined this Ur-Asa without him. He gave me all the raw material for the spells I put on him and the incantations I mumbled at his blue back descending the stairs, and then he acted as though it were my fault that he had to live up to an impossible standard.

Aşa, of course, did not invent me. Partly he was busy basking in my notion of him; partly my forthrightness left little room for speculation. He didn't need to translate me because what I said to him was unequivocal. I said, "I love you," and "You are the most delicious human in the world." His version of authorship was to list my qualities and marvel at them. "You're so, so—Italian." This, as we both knew, was a code word for Jewish.

What Jewishness meant to him was access to passion. He envied me that. I insisted that he could have passion, that my Jewish love would teach him how. But Gentile passions are reserved for moral issues, so the passion I aroused in Asa was ultimately a passion to do Right. And doing Right meant relinquishing me.

So there began the discrepancies. Between what he said and what I heard, between what he felt for me and what I felt for him, between how our office-mates thought of us and what was really going on, and, springing from that, between my reaction to secrecy and his: He wanted to maintain it, I wanted to blast it open. I thought if everybody knew, he'd leave Fay. In the end everybody did know. But I thoroughly misunderstood him. He had his own standard, one not fixed by public opinion. He was anything but amoral. Amorality was reserved for the Jews, like me and Reuben. We could be victims of our emotions; he knew what was right.

Toward the end there began to be discrepancies within me. I told myself that were he to leave Fay he would have proved himself untrustworthy and I wouldn't want him. I can't tell if I believed this. As I said, I became more like him, and this was a sentiment redolent of stern Yankee gobbledegook. On the other hand, it was true that an Asa who would ditch Fay and the dogs was no Asa I knew.

And the biggest discrepancy of all was between what we were and what we perceived in each other. Who did I love? What man was it who in my dreams and in the long vibrant winter evenings alone on my sofa I had kissed and awakened, feeding my images with conversations about layouts conducted in the fluorescence of the office? Whose eyes superimposed themselves on Fay's during dinner, halting his descriptions of his day at work? Can human beings love each other? Must we always love an image we've labored over secretly, never love the living soul with all its mire and murk?

ASA OBSERVED

Asa at fifty still dreams, but not of Dinah. At least, not often. Afternoon sunlight still finds a resting place at his feet on the desk. In his thoughts his feet walk the beaches of the Cape and the dimmer, dusty New Hampshire roads. The older he gets, Asa has noticed, the more he counts on summer to awaken him from a deepening winter slumber. It's as if he's turning into a bear. And so, bearish, he ambles warm paths that stretch into the infinitude of his imagination, shade whenever he wants it, beach roses at his side. Several long walks are needed to finish an article. They refresh him with their timelessness: He has no particular age while walking, and no sense of how many minutes, in the world of the office and the chair, they occupy. Enough, though, he figures, to warrant a discreet alarm system; he has installed a precarious lamp on a table outside his door, which wobbles and rattles at anyone's approach. He is amused that he's done this. Ten years ago he would have tried to cure himself of such serious woolgathering.

After nearly eighteen thousand days, Asa's life is peaceful. He has long since "gotten over" Dinah and returned his attention to his real life. But he does have another well-worn path to walk, which leads him back to all of that. He keeps it in his bottom drawer, beside a pint bottle of whiskey for emergencies. Not that he considers these two items as having the same value or effect. The whiskey rounds the edges; the hundred pages of his past sharpen them, clarify where the liquor soothes. Yet both seem to him on the order of vices, necessarily hidden. The occasional imperative to have a drink is slightly shameful, a lapse in good taste at the least. As to the other, it's hard for him to say what secret weakness his need for it reveals. But a few times a year—usually at the moment when the season changes, when winter first bites the soft heel of autumn, when drowsiness first overtakes the growth of leaves and they hang, fat and still, on the giant, ancient Cambridge trees—he opens what he thinks of as "his book."

And in her version of his life he has stopped looking for clues to himself. The first reading—years ago now—was a series of shocks: How could she know this, how not understand that; where had she gotten that idea? Most of all he'd wondered if that was, in fact, himself, the way he wondered about the oddly familiar, oddly repellent person in a tweed jacket reflected in storefront windows. He understands it now as a love poem of which he is only the accidental inspiration. Yet to be the subject, in some sense, of such a thing never stops surprising him and, though he is embarrassed to admit it, flattering him. He knows there is nothing flattering about it. He knows it is not even about him. But to the same degree as his features were once, to her eyes, contained in those of an angel in a painting he's never seen by an ancestor he never knew he had, so is his face discernible here. He is the model and he has the model's secret pride.

Asa is proud of something else these days as well. Over the last years, to make a little extra money, he has been writing articles about gardening for another magazine, also genteel, also tempered by dilettantism, more elegantly housed than his own magazine in a brownstone on the other side of the river. These articles are to be published as a book. He has conversations with an editor over tepid lunch in the Back Bay every six weeks; he will make even more money and, the editor assures him, a name for himself. Both the sum and the extent of his fame will be small, but Asa hasn't expected either. There will be photographs of his own and his favorite gardens. As an old hand in publishing, Asa knows the cost of color plates and is impressed. In fact, the plates more than any other aspect of the whole business have convinced him he is a success.

So one version of himself will appear in print. Asa believes in print. Print is not only the reality of his working day, it is a firm reality in itself. It endures, it is final, it is true. He does, in some way, still take soundings on life through literature. And he has resisted the middle-aged tendency to retreat to biographies. This year he has been rereading Hardy. Rather, reading Hardy, as *The Mayor of Casterbridge* gulped whole in one weekend at sixteen with *Return of the Native* for dessert the next week had been his entire exposure. Sometimes he shuts the book he's reading and looks at it, wondering that so much can be inside such an unprepossessing object. Other times he runs his fingertips across the pages to feel the letters; he has old editions, bought secondhand, cheap in broken sets.

But "his book"—her book—will never see print. He knows that now. When he first heard of it, when she told him about it in the Chinese restaurant, he feared Fay confronting him with a not-cryptic-enough dedication page, Roger smirking behind his desk, Cambridge abuzz again—for didn't Cambridge abound with *romans à clef,* whose demystification was the stuff of dinner parties?

Once a week they had gone to a Chinese restaurant in Central Square. Between a cut-rate shoe store and a Burger King, behind a plate-glass window opaqued by the old, the sad, the poor who waited at the bus stop, they ate pan-fried dumplings, beef with bean sauce, strange-flavored chicken. In lucky weeks they got a booth. By the cashier, carp swam in a muddy tank, round and round and round, as their conversations had begun to go round and round.

"I'm writing a book," she said, "about this."

"This—us?"

She nodded. "Well, you," she said.

"Have you changed the names?" he asked, and felt a fool.

"Of course," she said.

Their dumplings arrived and they ate. On that day they were not in a booth, so there was no handholding, no leaning across the table to see each other close and breathe each other's air. His rules: In retrospect they seemed both futile and mean. But what if someone had . . .

"Asa," she said. She so rarely addressed him by name that he swallowed his dumpling too quickly. It, or its shadow, lay like a rock in his throat, the sensation conjuring tears that were, on the whole, appropriate to his situation.

"Do you think you'll have another affair?"

He harrumphed to gain time and to urge the dumpling downward. "After you, you mean?"

"Yes."

"I don't know." She seemed so much, he could not then—or now—imagine embarking on it again.

"Have you thought about it?"

"Yes." A lie. He thought about it. Then, "I don't think I'm suited to it."

"No, you aren't." She assessed him. "But in some way—"

"I won't."

"Satisfied your curiosity about it?"

"It's not that." She shortchanged him somehow with this.

Then she was laughing, and the dumpling moved on, and she said, "Well, if you do have another, have it with me."

"Not that this one's over," he ventured, as much to soothe himself as her. "What is this book?"

"It's not really about us, it's more about you. But it's probably not about you either."

"When will you finish it?" He was being conversational,

but she went silent, sad, muffled by some rock of her own.

"I don't want to finish it," she mumbled.

"Then string it out," he said, easily.

"I'm terrified of finishing it."

How little he had given her. The burden of all she wanted, which was all he couldn't offer, pushed him to offer the only thing he had: more of what wasn't enough. "Finish it in the spring," he said to her. "That's a good time for beginnings."

"Beginning what?"

"A new life." And so committed himself to six more months of adultery.

In return, she put his fears of exposure to rest. "Remember when I went to Washington in the summer?" He did. She'd been away from work for three days. He'd missed her and had peace. "I went to Dumbarton Oaks. Have you been there?" He had, but only nodded. Whatever it was she was telling him, he was not going to interrupt with the rhodo-dendrons of Dumbarton Oaks. "Above the entrance to the courtyard there's a beautiful pediment with a Greek inscrip-tion, a long inscription. I wanted to know what it said, be-cause the courtyard was lovely, peaceful, and the doors were lovely, and the pediment—well, I went to find a guard, to see if he could tell me what it said. But on the wall opposite the courtyard I saw a card with the translation. It read: ART IS FOR MAN A HAVEN FROM SORROW. And it cheered me so. I hadn't known how sad I was, I think."

It was this therapeutic aspect he addressed when he asked her, from time to time, how the book was coming. For her part, Dinah was kind enough to say it was going well. It was still unfinished when she left—or so he has always assumed. She didn't give it to him until the next winter, and she had left, as agreed, in the spring.

It was late, late in the year when she called. The earth had frozen already and rang out under his feet when he walked to work: the hopeless month between Thanksgiving and Christmas.

"I have something for you," she said on the phone.

He feared it was a Christmas present. She'd given him two, and two birthday presents as well. He'd never given her anything. He dawdled on his way to the restaurant despite the cold, or maybe in hope of numbing himself further. He had by then achieved a blankness that, in moments of lucidity, he worried would be his permanent state.

Dumplings, spicy fish, rice for two; the moment had come to look at her. She looked the same. "Is that a new ring?"

"Asa, I've had this for fifteen years."

He did suddenly remember trying it on one summer afternoon and laughing because it didn't fit even his little finger. "Oh, yeah." He wanted a beer. Which was worse, forgetting or finding that wisp of memory?

"You're so unobservant," she said.

"Don't hold it against me." He raised his teacup. "Here's looking at you." He was, by then, able to more easily. It was true, she looked the same. "You never change."

"It's only been six months."

"I love the skin on this fish. Crackly." He realized she would think he was "avoiding" something.

But: "Very good," she agreed, and they discussed what seedlings were in his basement and Roger's latest unwritten article and how she was finding the free-lance life. He thought they might get through it without—what? Acknowledgment. And the longer they did, in fact, maintain their banal interchange, the safer he felt looking at her, enjoying her cheek and how it met her lip, the ivory of her sweater against her darker ivory neck, her hand clumsy with the chopsticks.

"You don't know how to use those," he told her. He realized she had always used them wrong. He moved to position them correctly for her. The sensation of her skin against his was so familiar that it was as if a landscape from boyhood were spread before his eyes. Her hand lay quiet in his. I've had a good life, he thought. He showed her how to cradle the sticks in the hollow between her thumb and forefinger; her hand was soft and pliant, and the whole time their skins brushed against each other he felt the warmth of his life surrounding him.

Then fortune cookies. "Why are they always like this? 'You have a good head for business.' " His was, "A friend asks only for your time and not your money."

"At least yours is true," she said.

"So what do you have for me?"

"What I wrote." She took a folder from her bag. "I wanted you to have a copy. After all, it's yours in a way. So here." She pushed it across the table.

They parted on the street, quickly, because it was cold and they didn't know how to say good-bye. They settled on an awkward hug made more ungainly by their coats and gloves. "Merry Christmas," they told each other, and "Let's not wait so long next time." Then they walked off in opposite directions.

It was a slow afternoon at work. The magazine had been put to bed the week before, and the pile of articles on Asa's desk was only thicker than it had been before he got caught up in the mechanics of the last issue. A profile of a physicist whose work he didn't understand; an article on weather; a photographic essay on East Africa. And on top, something by Dinah. Two-thirty. He cleaned his waxing machine. Three-ten. He discussed inside-cover advertising possibilities with the sales manager over the intercom. Three-twenty. He shut the door to his office. He put his feet on his desk and began to read.

It made him queasy, no doubt about it. He kept fighting the urge to stop. At the same time he was fascinated, because he saw himself there—but then again, *not* himself, a ghost or duplicate. The queasiness came from the way he felt shuttled between recognition and confusion. Several times he said out loud, "But it wasn't like that." And it hadn't been; surely he hadn't been such a wimp. Or was he then, and even now, and had she detected it? But he hadn't had anything to do with Reuben's girlfriend, who wasn't unlike Jo, surprisingly. He'd had a few ideas, maybe, but not . . . he had to keep reminding himself that this was a book. Or something, he didn't know exactly what. At any rate it was not his life history written down by someone else. Except that frequently it was.

How had she deduced that about the Breughel print? She must have seen it at the office Christmas party he gave two years before. But to make the leap to this piece of his adolescence—the one true tragedy he'd ever been involved in—was remarkable. Had he said something that gave her a clue? He poked his memory, but it seemed unreliable to him after the incident of her ring. Without her to prompt him, he might as well erase everything that had gone on between them. He saw himself, on the page and in the past, brooding at that picture as at a votive portrait. Perhaps, he thought, we are actually transparent to those who love us.

Six o'clock on a December evening; he was the last person in the building. At home Fay was lighting a fire for his welcome. She loved him too. There he was, in his warm, handsome office, holding a story written about him by a woman who loved him. All he had lost through death and neglect, and caution, and his damnable moderation—he did not think of it. Unassailable in his happiness, his luck in having received so much, he walked home through the night.

All these years, Asa has been too caught up in whether his book is "true" to know if it is "good." He has never even considered it from this angle. By now it is history: part of his life, an artifact he possesses. And though only a typescript, it, like Ovid and Hardy, is final and eternal.

As is Asa. Granite Asa, his substance does not change. Why did I think it could? If I could take an aerial photograph of Asa's rocky landscape, perhaps I'd find a new curve in a stream or a pile of stones freshly tumbled from a cliff—some slight evidence of my passage through the scene. But, reader, I can't get far enough away. I have never been able to. Asa is always in my middle distance at the least. I have held him closer and known less, but as yet I can move him no further from me.

Late at night when I look out my windows I see an apartment building. It is six stories high; behind it is Asa's house. I can't see Asa's house. For years this has frustrated me. Likewise has my inability to penetrate the lace of the branches that overshadow the Common, beneath which he walks to and from work each day. But I have come to realize that with nothing between us I was unable to see him. And so these physical impediments bother me less. They state the truth, which I am learning how to know.

I know who changed. I know whose soul awakened. I know whose blood these pages fanned to fire. I am sure of these things. For the rest, it is only hope, the whole world balanced on a straw. But on that straw we stake our lives and, heedless, we go on.

About the Author

Susanna Kaysen lives in Cambridge, Massachusetts, where she was born.

VINTAGE
CONTEMPORARIES

VINTAGE
CONTEMPORARIES

"Today's novels for the readers of today."

—VANITY FAIR

"Real literature—originals and important reprints—in attractive, inexpensive paperbacks."

—THE LOS ANGELES TIMES

"Prestigious."

—THE CHICAGO TRIBUNE

"A very fine collection."

—THE CHRISTIAN SCIENCE MONITOR

"Adventurous and worthy."

—SATURDAY REVIEW

"If you want to know what's on the cutting edge of American fiction, then these are the books you should be reading."
—UNITED PRESS INTERNATIONAL

On sale at bookstores everywhere, but if otherwise unavailable, may be ordered from us. You can use this coupon, or phone (800) 638-6460.

Please send me the Vintage Contemporaries books I have checked on the reverse. I am enclosing $_____ (add $1.00 per copy to cover postage and handling). Send check or money order—no cash or COD please. Prices are subject to change without notice.

NAME _____

ADDRESS_____

CITY _____ STATE_____ ZIP_____

Send coupons to:

RANDOM HOUSE, INC., 400 Hahn Road, Westminster, MD 21157

ATTN: ORDER ENTRY DEPARTMENT

Allow at least 4 weeks for delivery.